MERRY AND BRIGHT CHRISTMAS

BETTING ON CHRISTMAS

MEGAN RYDER

ABOUT MERRY AND BRIGHT CHRISTMAS

Sadie Taylor is not going to lose this bet. It's her best friend's wedding and if she doesn't have a date, the arrogant groomsmen win, and she won't ruin her friend's wedding like that.

With an abysmal dating life, Sadie visits a matchmaker that promises to find her soulmate. But fate has a twisted sense of humor. Sadie's perfect match is none other than Jaxon Bigsly, her high school boyfriend and love of her life.

No thanks. Been there, done that, and she still had the skid marks on her heart from the last time Jaxon left town.

Jaxon has always regretted leaving Sadie, but he's home now and plans to do more than settle in—he's going to win back the woman who still holds his heart.

But will the ghosts of the past make this a not so merry and bright Christmas?

CHAPTER ONE

SADIE

This could not be happening.

I wanted to sink through the hardwood floors here at The Bull and the Bear Tavern and fade away. But I had to settle for closing my eyes and praying that this was some horrible nightmare that I would wake up from. The silence in the tavern dining area was deafening, and when I opened my eyes again, it confirmed my worst fears. It was not a dream but a horrible reality that I was still living.

My date, the man I had been talking to for the past month and who I had such high hopes for, who seemed like a standup guy, was on his knees, blubbering like a baby. He had his arms wrapped around the thighs of a thin, blond woman. She was precariously balancing a tray of empty dishes, staring at him with horrified dismay, much like the rest of the crowd, to be honest. His words were barely discernible through the sobbing, but he was clearly pleading with her to take him back. That he couldn't live without her, that he loved her.

Just what a girl wanted to hear from the man she was dating. At least it was a first date. There certainly would not be a second one.

The waitress, Gina, going by her tag, gave me a wide-eyed, apologetic look, as if to say she had nothing to do with this. I shrugged and began looking around for our waitress, who most certainly had not been her, hoping to get the check or some escape route. Thank God I'd driven my own car. Single ladies always had an escape hatch for first dates, something drilled into me by my friends who had their share of first dates and insisted on this, along with the lifeline of telling each other where we went every time.

But it appeared everyone was avoiding the situation, just watching it like a scene from a horror movie. I was about to give up and throw money down on the table and run out when the manager came over. He said something, allowing Gina to extricate herself and flee. Lucky bitch. My date straightened and turned off the water works like they'd never happened.

He lifted his chair from the floor and set it back down at the table. He sat down and faced me. "How is your dinner?"

Like he had not just had a meltdown with his ex-girlfriend. What the actual…?

Clara Wilson, my employee, close friend, and instigator of the dating fiasco, almost fell off the stool in the kitchen in the back of my chocolate shop, Choco Dee Lites, laughing as I recounted the events of my date. I was doing what I always did when I was under stress, experimenting with a new recipe. Of course, I always needed to make more chocolate for the shop, but Clara had come in early to see how my date went and keep me company while I experimented with something new for my friend Chelsea Calhoun's wedding favors.

"Tell me you didn't stay after that!" Clara managed to get out between wheezes and tears of laughter.

I shot her a dirty look and continued to stir the chocolate.

"Of course not. But can you believe he was shocked that I wanted to leave? As if I would stay after he made a fool of himself over another woman. Apparently, this isn't the first time, though his ex apologized to me before I left."

"I hope you made him pay," Clara said, her eyes narrowing at me.

I avoided her look. "I wanted nothing to do with him. The manager comped my meal, though. They felt bad for me."

She shrugged and popped a piece of blueberry muffin from Brewed Awakenings in her mouth. "I wonder how many comped meals they've had to give from his dramatics."

"Don't know and don't care. But he's crossed off the list." I sighed and put the bowl down. "I had such high hopes for him. He had a job, lived on his own, seemed intelligent."

"Yeah, all qualities you look for in a date."

I registered her sarcasm, but chose to ignore it. "Exactly. Most importantly, he isn't someone I already know. Holly Creek is great, but I've known everyone here since they were toddlers. The dating pool is so small."

"Those aren't the only qualities you should be looking for."

I didn't want to tell her the real reason I was looking outside of Holly Creek. Everyone here reminded me of the one man who'd broken my heart. Hell, they still talked about him like he was my other half. "Well, he wasn't bad-looking."

Clara raised an eyebrow. "You're telling me that he looked like his picture?"

I bent my head and stirred the chocolate again. "Not exactly."

She hooted. "There you go. Online dating is not the place to look for a man. They lie on their profiles, and their pictures are always fake or touched up. It's all a lie."

"So why do you do it?"

She grinned a big Cheshire Cat grin. "Because Holly Creek has a small dating pool, and I need to find a date somewhere.

And I'm not as picky as you are. Seriously, Sadie, you have to be the pickiest woman I know!"

"Really? Having a job, living on your own, looking somewhat decent are not high qualities."

Clara swiped a spoon through the chocolate and tasted it, making a blissful face. "Yum. No, they're not high qualities. But they're not the only ones. You should be looking for romance, adventure, love. The other stuff sounds so boring."

"I had the other stuff, and it broke my heart."

Clara sighed. "I know, sweetie. But it's been ten years. Don't you think it's time to get back out there?"

"I will. I just need some time. Right now, all I need is a date to Chelsea's wedding. I can't go to that alone. It's bad enough that everyone feels bad for me about him." I refused to say his name. It was a constant reminder of the past. "But if I don't have a date, it makes it more obvious that I haven't moved on."

"You haven't," she gently reminded me. "And just *getting a date* won't work. It's not like the wedding is here in Holly Creek and you can meet up for the day. It's in the city, and you'll need to spend several days together, including sharing a hotel room, unless you want to ante up for a room for him, which will cost you plenty of bucks. And you have the bet to win."

I hated that she was right. A date for the wedding was not the best option, though I needed to hold up my end of the bridesmaids' bargain and make sure we didn't lose the bet with the groomsmen, those bunch of jerks. Unlike those guys from the city, none of us could afford to drop five hundred dollars for the bet and I couldn't dance for shit, not even on a stupid dance like the chicken dance. Besides it would embarrass our friend Chelsea, who had to make her new life among those city people.

Nope, we all had to find dates so we didn't lose the bet but, more importantly, it was time to move on, actually smarter to do what I'd said I was going to do: start dating for real. But with whom?

I must have said that out loud, because Clara frowned. "You could ask Courtney to set you up for a photoshoot."

I blinked. Courtney? This was what Clara thought I should do to find a man? Resort to an intimate couples' photo shoot with a stranger? A boudoir photo shoot?

Clara stared back at me as if she were nothing but serious, and I immediately shook my head, nerves twisting in my belly at the mere thought.

My friend, Courtney Maddux, was a goddess with a camera. Absolutely brilliant. She took amazing photographs, whether doing her stranger-boudoir photo shoots, where she took two complete strangers and put them together for an intimate moment or several and capturing them on film. Or if she was wrangling a family of five, all in matching beige or denim clothing for a holiday card or family event. Hell, she even took pictures of our many events in Holly Creek, bringing in more people just by her pictures. I didn't care that tourists were known for showing up for the express purpose of hoping to be chosen as one of Courtney's subjects. Nor that an unexpected number of the previously unknown couples she paired together ended up dating. Some had even married. I was not doing that. I was not putting my curvy, a little-too-large backside—who was I kidding, all sides—on display for a camera while also snuggling "all this" up against a stranger.

"No," I finally managed when Clara simply continued to peer at me.

She shrugged. "I had to ask. Courtney has a reputation for putting people together."

"No," I said again, a little more forcefully this time and refocused on my task. I wasn't sure I could do a boudoir shot, even if I'd been in a steady relationship for years.

"Then you could finally go out with Devon Paxton."

"Already did that." I shuddered at the memory. "Disaster."

Clara straightened, and in the next instant, a squeal shot out of her. "You went out with Devon? You're kidding! You never told me. You must be desperate."

I sighed and sat on the stool, abandoning my chocolate. "Because it was a disaster. He and Jax never got along, and he spent the entire night comparing himself to Jax and how I was much better off without Jax."

Clara eyes went wide. "What a douche. He spent the entire night ranting about your ex? Maybe he has a thing for him."

"Oh, he has a thing all right, and not a good thing. He hates Jax, and I didn't need the constant reminder." I shook my head. "That's how all my dates with guys from Holly Creek go. Asking about Jax. Reminiscing about the good old days with Jax. How he and I were the golden couple. No, I can't relive that. I need a fresh start."

She nodded as if this was what she'd been waiting for. "Perfect. This will be the opportunity for you to find the right person and finally move on."

I threw up my hands. "What do you think I've been doing? I tried dating locally. Then I tried online dating, and I get the losers and those still hung up on their exes. What's next?"

"How about a matchmaker?"

I froze, my coffee halfway to my mouth. "A matchmaker? Like when my mother set me up with her bridge partner's son? If you recall, that was a disaster."

Clara smirked. "Yeah, no. Not like that. A professional matchmaker who helps you find your soul mate."

"I don't need a soul mate. I need a date to the wedding. That's all."

"Why settle for that when you can have both?"

We had been talking about moving on. This could help me finally cut my ties to the past. I certainly hadn't been successful on my own. I had spent most of my time building my business, though I admit that had been an excuse not to date. But my chocolate shop was finally doing well, and I could start to look for the next phase of my life. Settling down to the family I'd always wanted.

"How would that work? I don't know of any matchmakers in Holly Creek, except the busybodies and my mother. Well, and you."

Clara grinned and handed me her phone. "There's this festival a few times a year that happens in Lovelorn, a couple of hours from here, in the Finger Lakes region. It's gorgeous there, and they have their own matchmaker. The festivals are where he helps people find their soul mates. Now you can sign up to meet with the matchmaker and enlist his help or just meet people, hoping to find someone on your own. I suggest you sign up for him."

She paused, her teeth nibbling at her lower lip. "Don't be mad, but I may have already submitted your application."

I stared at her, the words barely penetrating my brain. "What do you mean, you already submitted my application?"

"Okay, look. I knew that guy was going to be a loser. He was an accountant, okay? Come on. He would never be right for you. He was safe. You need someone you could actually fall for. You would never fall for him. So I submitted the application online. And good thing I did. There are two more festivals, one more next week and another in September."

"I can't go in September. It's our busiest time."

She smiled, a gleam in her eye. "Exactly. September is too busy. You'd never give anyone a chance. But you can go next week and meet someone, have plenty of time to get to know them before the wedding, and maybe fall in love!"

CHAPTER TWO

JAXON

The one thing I would not miss about Lovelorn was the tourist traffic during festival season. Nor would I miss the single women looking for love, propositioning every guy who passed by, hoping one of them was their soul mate.

Sorry, ladies. I already found my soul mate and fucked it all up.

I weaved through the small crowd at The Happy Hookup with a case of our latest ale from the Brimstone Fermentary, Infernal Ale. It was my special recipe that I had been perfecting with hops grown in the region. I hoped to enter the national contest, pending how it went over this week at the festival. Of course, if all went well, I'd have another brew I could enter the contest from my own brewery, too.

Drew Cafferty, owner of The Happy Hookup, waved me over to the back side of the bar. "Jaxon! Is this the new ale you've been bragging about for the past few months?"

"Yup. I'd appreciate hearing what you and your customers think about it."

He opened one of the bottles and poured a glass. He took a deep inhale, then sipped the beer. "Nice flavor, Jax. Not too heavy, but a good heft to it. Refreshing too. Both our male customers and many of our women will like it. It's a nice balance between the heavy and light. You nailed it with this one."

I grinned, a weight lifted from my shoulders. Drew might be considered an easygoing joker among many people, but I knew he was serious about his bar and what he served. He didn't bull-shit people about his beer. "Thanks, Drew. I have more cases in the truck."

"Awesome. Let me give you a hand." He clapped me on the back and followed me out the back of the bar.

As we headed for the truck, he said, "Is it true that you're leaving?"

I paused, hand on the door of the truck. "Where did you hear that?"

He shrugged. "You know how gossip mills work in small towns. Someone heard it from someone else. I heard you might be leaving for another brewery. Buying your own."

Damn it. How had word gotten around so quickly? "I put in an offer a few months ago with a buddy of mine. We are working through the details now. Nothing is official."

Drew only grinned affably. "No worries. I won't say anything. We'll miss you if it's true. But if it is, know that I'd be happy to carry your brew here anytime. And I wish you all the best."

I could feel my shoulders relax. Lovelorn was a small town, but it had a thriving tourist trade. I had hoped to use my connections to expand distribution into this town once I got operations up and running. Our offer had been accepted just that morning, but I wasn't going to share that news with Drew. I first had to discuss it with my business partner and college friend, Sean Wallace, then I had to give notice to Eric James at Brimstone. Not only did I work for them, but this was their territory, though Drew carried a lot of other beers in the bar. I didn't want to put him in an awkward position or burn any bridges with Brimstone. He'd been good to me, teaching me how to be the best brewmaster I could be. Now I was ready for my own brewery, and the owners had given their blessing, along with advice and help. I couldn't be more grateful.

I loved my job with Brimstone, but it was time for me to move on with my plans. When I heard that Tap Meister was up for sale finally, it was like the last piece of the puzzle had slotted into place. I had left Holly Creek after high school like everyone else, but instead of returning like I had planned, something inside of me broke, and I ran. I ran from my family, the expectations, and from the only woman I'd ever loved.

I wouldn't say it was a mistake. The pressure of living in Holly Creek, a small town who placed such high expectations on my shoulders, had gotten to be too much for me. And my father couldn't seem to understand that I wasn't him, that I didn't want the things he wanted or, worse yet, was terrified to live the life he had, peaking in high school, never accomplishing anything more than being a high school football star, then falling on a steady decline ever since. And it wouldn't just be me that I would take down. Sadie Taylor would be right by my side, the perfect woman, who would one day resent the hell out of me. I couldn't watch that love turn to hate or worse, disinterest.

I needed to leave to breathe and find myself, but I regret how I left things. Now I was going back, now that I knew who I was and was confident in myself, and I hoped I hadn't destroyed everything.

Drew was watching me with a quizzical look on his face. "Everything all right?"

I pasted on a smile. "Yeah, let's get this unloaded. Thanks."

I had decisions to make and plans to put into motion.

When I got back to Brimstone, my boss and owner of the brewery, Eric, was waiting for me in my office. We didn't have a meeting that I knew of, and he was just scrolling through his phone, so I wasn't alarmed. Not really.

"Eric, sorry to keep you waiting. Did we have a meeting?"

Eric was an older man, mid-fifties, with a neatly trimmed salt and pepper beard and hair. He was fit and stayed in shape by working around the brewery and on the farm he owned, where we grew the hops for our beer, along with other crops. He wasn't the type to sit still for long or spend time on a golf course. He was a worker, spending his time alongside his employees, not in an office or overseeing everyone. So it wasn't unusual to see him in my office, just unexpected.

Eric stood and shook my hand, then we both sat. "You delivered the Infernal Ale? Don't we have drivers for that?"

I shrugged. "I wanted Drew's reaction myself. He seemed to like it."

Eric nodded. "It's a good recipe. I think it will be a staple in our line-up for years to come. You did a good job with it. That's one of the reasons I'm here."

I waited patiently. Eric rarely doled out praise unless it was deserved, but his words were intriguing. "Thank you. We've worked hard for the right balance."

He nodded. "I hear congratulations are in order. They've accepted your offer?"

"How did you know?"

Hell, I had only heard that morning and was still waiting to talk with my business partner and college friend, Sean, before saying anything to anyone else. How had Eric heard already?

He grinned. "The brewery business is a small world, especially with another brewery only a few hours away and in the same state. Congratulations, Jaxon. You've worked hard for this."

He lifted a bottle of champagne from the floor and two glasses. He poured the champagne, and we toasted. I sat back in my chair, finally relaxing. I had been nervous to tell Eric I was leaving, even though he knew about the offer and had even offered advice about my business plan, but as usual, he made it easy.

He watched me, a shrewd expression on his face. "Are you ready for this step?"

He wasn't asking about the brewery, though that was a significant business and financial risk. He'd help advise us on securing the investment and capital for the investment, but he knew this move was not solely about Sean and me buying our brewery and making that dream a reality. It was about returning home, righting some past wrongs, and seeing if I could fix one of the biggest mistakes I'd ever made.

I shrugged, taking a bigger swallow of the champagne that I had wanted, choking a little on the bubbles. "I'll have to be, won't it? I can't take it back."

"You could always retract the offer. You haven't signed the papers. And you'll always have a job here. Though Charlie might be disappointed to not take over as brewmaster."

We laughed. Charlie had been my assistant for the past couple of years, a man older than me and more than ready to take over. "He'll be fine. No, I'm ready for this. It's past time I go home again. My sister has a couple of kids now. She wants her brother around so her kids can know their Uncle Jax. And my dad isn't getting any younger and could use some help around the house, too." Not that my dad would appreciate my help. He never did, not after I broke his heart by not playing football in college and pursuing a professional career.

"They're only a couple of hours away. It's not like you're a continent away from them," Eric pointed out, pouring more champagne into both of our glasses.

It was more than my family, and he knew it. I was going

back for her, for the one who got away. Sadie Taylor. Though she might not welcome me back, not the way I'd left things with her. In fact, she might hate me, maybe have even moved on. Was I prepared for that? My sister had refused to talk about her, even though I knew they had remained good friends. Lila told me that she wouldn't betray her friendship with Sadie by giving me information about her friend, only that I should man up soon or I might lose my shot.

Personally, I think I blew my shot when I didn't go back to Holly Creek after college, as Sadie and I had planned. I only hoped that I was wrong and Sadie could forgive me and give me a second chance. Or else it would be hell watching her move on with someone else. And I wouldn't be able to do anything about it, owning a business in town.

"No, this is the right choice. I'm excited about this next step."

Eric smiled and lifted his glass. "Then I'm happy for you. Sad to lose you, but happy for you. What about Germany? Will that change anything?"

I sobered. "I haven't heard anything about Germany. There's still time. They said they wouldn't select their final candidates until the fall, but I had hoped to know something by now. Sean says he'll be fine if I get the internship."

"Best of luck to you. And you can always reach out if you have questions."

We finished our champagne and reviewed the plans for the handoff. I ignored the niggling feeling that Eric triggered in me. I had a plan, and it would work. I'd go home to Holly Creek, take over Tap Meister, and win Sadie back. Everything else would sort itself out.

CHAPTER THREE

SADIE

I should have made Clara come with me. This was her crazy-ass idea, and I should have forced her to suffer alongside of me. Or instead of me. Only she would have enjoyed every minute of this, soaking up the male attention, finding enough dates to hold her through the holiday season.

Clara was three years older than me and loved being in her dating phase, not quite looking for Mister Right, but more interested in Mister Right-Now. She had come to town a couple of years ago and had struck up a friendship with my good friend, Lila Bigsly Addison. When Clara needed a job, Lila recommended my shop. I needed a friendly counter salesperson so I could focus on my recipes. Clara was a godsend in those early days, and the three of us became good friends, even if Lila was he-who-shall-not-be-named's younger sister. I forgave her for her accident of birth, and we moved on without ever mentioning him.

Clara was not ready to settle down and was happy to date. She was slightly plump—more to love, as she called it—and a cheerful sort that charmed customers into buying more chocolate than they expected. She saw the good in everything but had a ruthlessly practical side I valued. She would have loved Lovelorn. The adorable shops. The vendors all set up on the town green. The bar, appropriately named The Happy Hookup. And all the men looking for their soul mate.

I found it hard to believe all these men were looking for true love. Some of them had to be looking to score. The town was packed with people, single and ready to mingle. Everywhere you went, it was one big singles mixer. I had heard some very interesting opening lines, and none of them were typical of a bar hookup, which was refreshing.

Currently, I was enjoying a drink, a Bee's Knees that was made perfectly, at a table by the window of the very quaint and adorable bar The Happy Hookup, and watching the crowd mix around me. My appointment with the matchmaker, thank you Clara, wasn't for another two hours. Instead of hiding in my room, which I wanted to do, I'd decided to put herself out there. I had promised Clara and Lila that I'd take a chance this week and see what happened.

A shadow fell across my table. I glanced up to see a tall, sandy-haired man, slightly older than me, standing there, looking a little hesitant. "Hi, I'm Marcus. I couldn't help but notice you sitting here by yourself. I hope I'm not intruding, but I thought I'd come over and introduce myself."

Well, that wasn't a pickup line, and he seemed friendly, if a little shy. I gestured to the seat across from me. "Sure. That would be nice."

He had a pleasant smile, easy and kind. A lock of hair fell over one eyebrow, giving him a boyish charm and making him appear younger than what I guessed was around early to mid-thirties. He glanced at my drink. "Do you want another?"

I laughed. "Oh no, thanks. One is my limit, at least for now. I want to pace myself."

He nodded. "That's smart. Are you from the area?"

I shook my head. "Not exactly. I'm from a few hours away. I'm a tourist, I'm afraid. A first-timer. You?"

He smiled again, that broad, friendly smile. "Oh, I'm from Syracuse. I come down as often as I can. They have the best vineyards in the region. My buddies and I like to visit in the summer. There are a lot of fun things to do. One of my buddies has a boat."

"That sounds like fun," I replied, taking a sip of my drink.

"It is." He launched into a recitation of the activities he and his buddies did all summer. It sounded a little more like a group of frat boys than thirty-something men to me, but maybe I was wrong. Who was I to judge what single men did when they were on vacation?

I glanced at his hand wrapped around the glass of beer and something caught my eye. I almost missed his words. "I'm sorry. What did you say?"

"Do you want to come out on the boat tomorrow? It's going to be a great day. We're going to go water-skiing."

I gestured to his hand. "Wouldn't your wife mind?"

His face turned red, and he curled his hand onto his lap. "We're separated."

Not long enough for the tan line to have faded. "No, thanks."

His smile faded to something like anger. He stood. "Fine. I'm sure I'll find someone else. There are plenty of women around."

I waved my hand for him to leave, but he was already gone. Yeah, there were always men looking to score. A man came over and dropped off the club sandwich I'd ordered and a glass of water. He paused, as if waiting for something.

I looked up, and he smiled. "Not everyone is like that guy. Most people here are genuine."

I blinked, startled by his comment. "Thank you. How did you know?"

He grinned. "I'm Drew Cafferty. I own the place. The matchmaker is my grandfather. My brother and I keep an eye on the people here. The guy who came over is Steve Wilson. We know him, and when he starts his moves on women, we gently encourage him to go elsewhere."

I raised an eyebrow. "So he is married."

"Yup, and his wife knows about his partying. No idea why she tolerates it. Maybe to get a weekend free." He winked and walked away.

"Excuse me. I saw you at the Nestled Inn this morning. Do you mind if I join you?" A woman's voice broke into my lunch, and I looked up.

A familiar face from that morning looked hopefully at me. Her dark hair was pulled back in a simple ponytail, and she looked as overwhelmed as I felt. "Absolutely. Please."

She sank into the chair with a sigh of relief. "Thank you. My sister encouraged me to come to this, saying it would be the ideal place to meet someone, but I confess, I didn't expect it to be so much."

I laughed, already feeling comfortable with her. "My friend did the same for me. She even sent in my application for the matchmaker. Frankly, I'm nervous."

"Well, I'm Theresa. Nice to meet you, nervous."

I rolled my eyes but grinned. "I'm Sadie. Nice to meet you too. Are you staying for the week?"

Theresa leaned forward. "I'm terrified. And yes, my sister filled out my application for me, too. I can only imagine what she put on there. My appointment is later today. You?"

"In an hour. I already warned my friend that if she put down anything that's wrong or I don't like, she'd better not be in town when I get back."

She sat back and laughed. "I wish I had your guts. My sister would ignore me. I know she only wants to help, but does she realize how scary this is?"

"Right? I should have made Clara come with me. This is like the worst and biggest singles bar ever." I paused. "Let's make a pact. Let's help each other through the week and not let anything bad happen. Deal?"

She took my hand, a look of relief on her face. "Deal. Maybe now I can eat something. Drinking on an empty stomach can't be good for you."

I gestured for the waitress. "Tip number one. Avoid this guy named Steve Wilson. He's married and a player."

Her eyes widened, and she leaned forward as I told the story.

All too soon, my hour was up, and it was time for my appointment. Theresa saw me off with an encouraging word and a comforting squeeze of the hand. She stayed at the table to hold it, and I hoped she didn't have Steve or any of his friends hit on her while I was gone. She was a nice girl, and way kinder than I was. Though a guy at the bar had already been making eyes at her, and she was looking back, so I suspected my seat would be taken by the time I made it back from the interview. He seemed decent, and I didn't see a ring, so I hoped that he was one of the good guys.

I made my way to the other side of the bar, to a half circular corner booth where an older man sat. Despite the crowd in the bar, everyone gave the booth a wide berth, as if knowing this was a private space. The man was close to eighty at least, with a full head of white hair. He was thin, slender, and not very tall, maybe my height or a little taller, around five foot eight or nine inches. His face was kind with laugh lines around his mouth and eyes. He was a man that you could see yourself opening up to, one that encouraged confidences.

He sat by himself, and I stopped, waiting for him to acknowledge me. He looked up with bright blue eyes. "Miss Taylor, I believe?"

I nodded and slid into the booth across from him as directed. "Yes, Sadie Taylor. You're William Quinn?"

He nodded. Before we could continue speaking, a woman and Drew showed up. The woman slid in next to William and Drew next to me after handing William a glass of what appeared to be whiskey. William took a sip and sighed.

"Thank you, Drew. I needed that. Matchmaking is thirsty business." He focused on me. "This is my granddaughter, Colleen, who helps me with the matching. And you may have met my grandson Drew, who is learning the family business."

Drew gave me a wink and a heart-pounding grin while Colleen nodded and pulled out a folder and papers, handing them to William. "Her application, Granddad."

He waved them aside. "Let's spend some time talking first. I'd like to get to know you, Sadie."

Colleen gave a little sigh, as if she'd expected this. Three sets of eyes focused on me, and I panicked. "I don't know what you want to know. I'm twenty-eight. I own my own chocolate shop. I'm single, obviously. And my friends thought this would be a good way to meet someone."

William's eyes twinkled, and he reached across the table and patted my hand. "A chocolate shop sounds delightful. Colleen might want your details, or maybe Drew. They both have a sweet tooth."

"Maybe we could have you come for our Valentine's Day festival. It's smaller, more intimate, but your chocolates would be wonderful, and it won't be as hot as summer," Colleen suggested.

I had walked around the vendors' tents and thought about asking how I could get a spot for one of the festivals someday. Here was an opportunity being dropped in my lap. I dug in my handbag for a brochure and my business card, because I never went anywhere without them. "That would be perfect. Here is my contact information."

Colleen took them and began flipping through the brochure. Now I wished I had brought some of my chocolate as samples. Clara had pushed me out the door and refused to let me think about work, saying this was a vacation. But as a business owner, there was never such a thing as a true vacation.

William took a sip of his whiskey. "So how long have you been single, Sadie?"

"I've dated, but no one regularly. Not since high school. I've been focused on my career, to be honest. Culinary school, internship, then the shop. Dating wasn't a priority."

William took another sip and waited, as if he sensed there was more. I took a deep breath and took the plunge. "Here's the thing. I had a serious boyfriend in high school and in college. I thought we were going to get married, but we weren't on the same page at all about what we wanted out of life."

The older man nodded sagely. "High school is awfully young to have met the love of your life. Many kids think they have it all figured out only to realize that it's not what they wanted after all."

I squirmed on the wooden booth. These words were exactly what Jax had said to me when he broke things off, saying that we were too young to know what we really wanted.

"Respectfully, everyone told me that back then, and ten years later, I still want the same things. A shop of my own. A family. A life in my small town. I'm not asking for the world. Just someone who wants to live a quiet life in a small town and have a family. If he wasn't ready for that, then it was better that he moved on."

William leaned forward and took my hand. "Those aren't unreasonable requests, though location might be something you may need to compromise on. Have you been open to people in your town?"

"I love Holly Creek. My family and my business are there. I can't move."

"You could move, but you choose not to. You understand that this may limit your choices, correct?"

I nodded, knowing that was a real problem. Leaving Holly Creek wasn't an option. I loved my town, and I had a business there now. It was home. I never wanted to live anywhere else. This had been one of the major issues between Jaxon and me, although clearly there were others. He hadn't wanted to stay in Holly Creek either, despite being loved by almost everyone there. In fact, he couldn't wait to shake the town's dust off his feet. He'd rarely been back, and I'd been able to avoid him, thanks to some judicious travel plans when his sister Lila had warned me he was coming home for a visit. Her wedding had been the only thorn, but she understood when I had to miss it. I felt terrible, but I couldn't face him. She'd chosen a destination wedding to minimize the impact. Where had that been?

"I understand. Honestly, I only really need a date for a wedding at the holidays. A relationship would be nice, though."

And it would be. I was ready to move on to the next phase, ready to settle down and have someone in my life. I was tired of being lonely, spending my time watching television alone, eating alone, and working all the time. Just once, I'd like to have a date, someone to make plans with, wake up with in the morning. Hell, I didn't even have a pet. Maybe I should start with the local animal shelter before I tracked down a boyfriend, see if I could handle someone else in my space. A cat or dog wouldn't complain about living in Holly Creek. They'd be happy to have a home.

"Oh, I think we can do better than just a date. Most of our festival attendees are regional, so they shouldn't be too far from your home. Let's look at your application and get to know each other a little better, shall we?"

❄

By the time I finished my interview with William, I was wrung out. Drew escorted me from the table, a hand on my lower back, over to where I had been sitting. Surprisingly, my chair was empty and Theresa was waiting. She looked up expectantly with a broad smile when she saw me, which turned to alarm.

"Oh my God, are you okay?"

I sank into the chair and ordered a drink. This was definitely a two-drink afternoon. Drew grinned and headed for the bar. "It was intense. Fair warning. William Quinn looks like a sweet old man, but he is a shark when it comes to asking questions. I think he was an interrogator for the CIA in a past life."

Theresa looked alarmed and began chewing on her lower lip. "Thanks for the warning. Now I'm even more nervous."

Drew dropped another Bee's Knees at my table. "Relax. You did fine."

I huffed a laugh and took a healthy swallow of my drink. "So anything interesting happen while I was gone?"

Theresa's face went tomato red, and she glanced toward the bar. A sweet young man stood there with a couple of other men, glancing her way every so often, a shy smile on his face. She leaned forward. "His name is Michael, and he's here for the festival. I don't think he's doing the whole interview thing, but he seems nice."

I looked over and let my gaze travel over him. He was wearing Dockers and a blue button-down shirt and boat shoes. His friends were dressed similarly, nothing ostentatious, and they were acting low-key. They seemed like decent enough guys. The way he kept stealing looks over at the table was kind of cute, and I was happy for her.

"He seems nice," I offered, though my words seemed lame.

Her smile broadened. "He asked me to dinner tonight. Do you think I should go?"

"Why not? You're here to meet people. Go, have fun."

She stood up, and Michael came over, a shy smile on his face. And they left the bar together, their heads close as they chatted. Looked like I was eating alone tonight. The diner seemed to have a nice menu. I'd give that a shot and head back to the room for an early evening.

"Sadie? Sadie Taylor? Is that you?"

It couldn't be. After all these years. I had to be hearing things, especially after thinking about him all day. The power of suggestion or some such bullshit.

I slowly shifted in my seat and looked up. Oh my God. Jaxon Bigsly. Here in Lovelorn. What were the odds? I was going to kill Lila.

CHAPTER FOUR

JAXON

After I had confirmed that our offer had been accepted and spoken with my partner, Sean, I wanted to celebrate. Only the people I would celebrate with were either those I worked with or were hanging out at The Happy Hookup in town. And it was festival week, so the bar was going to slammed. But it didn't matter. I was going home, finally.

When I walked in, I couldn't believe my eyes. Over in an alcove sat the woman I had been dreaming of for the past eight years. The woman for whom this whole venture was designed. Sadie Taylor. What the hell was she doing in Lovelorn?

Sadie had been the cute cheerleader and class president in high school. Honey-blond hair pulled back in a ponytail, bright, cheery smile, beautiful hazel eyes that sparkled when she talked. There may have been more beautiful women, but she was always the one for me. Now she took my breath away. She'd grown into a gorgeous woman with curves in all the right places. Her hair had darkened to the color of a honey ale that had been brewed in the fall, yet her face still had that soft, gentle, warmth I remembered. She always made me feel like I was coming home and yet lit a fire in me that had never died.

My blood heated in an instant, remembering how she felt in my arms, how it was to kiss her plump lips or taste her sweet skin, which always had a hint of chocolate or sugar. My body, which I had feared was in hibernation, wakened and demanded that I see if she tasted as good as I remembered, but her warning expression gave me pause.

Judging by the shocked and horrified look on her face, my sister hadn't told her that I was working in Lovelorn. *Damn it, Lila.*

Before Sadie could make her escape, I was standing in front of her. "Please, Sadie. Don't go. Not yet. What are you doing here?"

She glared, that fire in her hazel eyes snapping at me, reminding me of the chocolate she'd loved to make even back in high school. "I could ask you the same thing. What are you doing here?"

"I work here at Brimstone Fermentary as the brewmaster."

The look of betrayal on her face tore at my heart, like a knife to my gut. She winced as if my words caused her physical pain. "How long?"

I could barely hear her over the noise of the crowd, but the pain in her voice came through clearly. "Three years."

She closed her eyes for a moment, then opened them, unshed tears shining. "Why didn't Lila tell me you were only a couple of hours away? Did you hate me, Holly Creek, that much that you couldn't even come home when you were that close?"

"It was never about hating Holly Creek or you, Sadie. Look, can we go somewhere quieter to talk?"

She shook her head, recoiling a little in her seat as if to protect herself. "I don't think that's a good idea, Jaxon. I think you should just leave me alone."

I hooked my ankle around a spare chair and dragged it over, taking her hand as I sat down. "Sadie, please. I really want to explain. Have you had dinner yet?"

I held my breath, hoping she'd give me this chance. I also didn't want her around the people who could tell her that I was returning to Holly Creek. It was too soon to break that news to her. I hadn't told anyone from back home, not even my family. It needed to be a surprise in case something fell through. Until everything was official, I wanted to keep that news under wraps.

But I could at least try to find closure with Sadie and see if I had a chance with her. A chance to make things right.

Finally, she nodded, a small one, without looking at me. It was tentative, as if she wasn't sure she should go, but it was a start. And I would take any chance I had with her, hoping that I could wedge that door open again and find my way back inside.

I stood and held out my hand. "Over Easy is the local diner. They usually only serve breakfast and lunch, but during festival season, they're open for dinner. They have great food. Reminds me a bit of Flora's back home."

A ghost of a smile curved her lips. "I love that place. I was thinking of going to Over Easy for dinner, anyway."

"Great. We can beat the dinner rush, well, except for the senior citizens." I winked and she barely smiled back, but I'd take it. She wasn't all in, but I had a chance.

Now to not blow it.

We settled in a booth toward the back of Over Easy. Hazel Stewart, one of the owners, had taken our order, giving Sadie a quizzical look, then an eyebrow raise to me. I had never brought a girl in here, except my sister, and Hazel was one of the leading gossip mavens in town. This news would make the rounds by bedtime. I couldn't find it in myself to care about the gossip or what they said. I'd deal with that tomorrow. Tonight, I had some groveling to do.

"So what brings you to Lovelorn?"

Sadie had spent most of the initial part of our evening studying the menu, then the paper placemat with advertisements for local businesses. She had yet to look at me, so I didn't know what she was thinking. Was she angry, upset, or attracted to me? Honestly, I could deal with any of those emotions because it would mean she felt something for me. If she was indifferent, then I might have already lost her, and signing the papers to Tap Meister would be a waste of my time.

She finally looked me square in the eye. "I could lie and say I'm here for a vacation, but we'd both know that wasn't true. It's festival season, so I'm here for the matchmaker. I need a date for my friend's wedding and hoped to find one here, and maybe a soul mate at the same time."

I had suspected that, but hearing it was a kick to the gut. Once upon a time, I'd thought I was her soulmate, but then I broke her trust, shattering our bond when I left her. Would she take me back now, or would she look for someone new? I struggled against my instinct to demand that she give up the notion and be mine again. I had to play this cool and not be an asshole about it. I had to earn back her trust.

"William Quinn is a good man and a reputable matchmaker. Have you met with him?"

For the first time, her face lit up with a smile of genuine pleasure. "I did, earlier today, along with his grandson and granddaughter, Drew and Colleen. He's very thorough, asking a lot of questions about what I was looking for, my past dating life, and what I want now. My assistant actually filled out the application, not me, so I wasn't sure what she'd put on there. But she apparently knows me pretty well."

I raised an eyebrow. "You don't seem happy about that."

She wrinkled her nose, an endearing trait I had forgotten about. "It's not that I'm not happy about it. I just hadn't realized how transparent I was about what I wanted or who I was. I guess I can scratch sexy and mysterious off my list of qualities for my dating profile."

I couldn't help but reach for her hand. "I wouldn't scratch them off just yet. You're still as sexy as you were back when we were dating."

She pulled her hand away and buried it in her lap under the table. "Don't say things like that, Jaxon. If you had cared about me, you wouldn't have broken up with me."

I fisted my hand but pulled it back. "I disagree. I did what I thought was best for both of us. We wouldn't have done half the things we'd wanted to do if we had stayed together in Holly Creek. We needed time to grow up, time to grow into who we are."

The excuse wasn't a complete lie. We'd needed time to grow up. Both of us had things to accomplish. How could I tell her that I couldn't take the pressure the town had placed on me? That maybe I wasn't the golden boy everyone wanted to believe? Bringing our team to the state championship was one of the best and worst things I ever did it my life. I'd heard it all from everyone, especially my dad, the plans they all had for me. But no one ever asked me what I wanted.

She narrowed her eyes at me. "Maybe you did, but I was able to accomplish everything I wanted while still living there. Sure, I went to culinary school downstate and took some internships to round out my skills, but I always had my home. And you didn't exactly travel very far. Lovelorn is only a few hours away. What you wanted was time away from me."

"It was never you, Sadie. It was always me."

I didn't know how to explain that to her. Hell, I couldn't even explain it to myself. I just needed to leave Holly Creek and the stifling expectations that threatened to bury me. Unlike Sadie, who thrived under them, I felt like they would swamp me, destroy me under their weight until I broke and everyone saw the real me, the failure that I was or that I was destined to be. I could never achieve those lofty goals. I had to escape and find out who I was before I could deal with that pressure.

She snorted. "Oh, the *it's not you, it's me* line. Save it, Jaxon. I don't need to hear it. I've lived it. You're right. It was you. I'm happy with my choices. I love my town. I love my life. If you couldn't see the treasure we had, then I feel sorry for you." She stood. "But I want to thank you. I never felt like I had closure after our breakup. I always felt like there was something missing, incomplete. But now I'm finally ready to move on. And I'm in the perfect place for it."

She walked around the booth and pressed her lips to my cheek. "Have a good life, Jaxon. Goodbye."

And she walked out, leaving me behind, as I had once done to her.

CHAPTER FIVE

SADIE

I cried that night, cried again for losing Jaxon, but it felt cathartic, as if I had finally let go of the past. It was like I told Jaxon at dinner. I had never felt like I had closure, and now I did. Now I was ready to let someone else in. Hopefully, William Quinn had found my soul mate and could introduce me. Frankly, I would be surprised if he found someone that quickly or if the planets had aligned to place that one person on Earth who was perfect for me in Lovelorn at this moment. I hadn't been this lucky before. Why would today be different?

Yet when I woke up this morning in my incredibly comfortable bed at the Nestled Inn, my eyes gritty and dry from crying but my soul infinitely lighter, I had a flashing text message from William Quinn. He asked me to meet him that afternoon in the park. It was going to be a lovely day, and he didn't want to be inside.

I sat propped up against the headboard with my pillows as cushions and thought about the message and whether I was truly ready. The sun streaming between the floral curtains seemed to signify a new day had dawned, cleansing me of everything that had gone before. I took a deep breath and somehow felt lighter. Yes, I was ready.

There was a light knock at the door. "Yes?"

"Sadie? I was going to grab some breakfast and take a walk around the lake. Did you want to join me?"

Theresa's voice came through the door, and I remembered we had talked about that walk the previous day. "Let me take a quick shower. I'm running a bit behind. Be down in twenty. Save me a muffin!"

It didn't take me long to get ready, and Theresa was almost bouncing in her seat in excitement after her dinner date the previous evening. After a quick breakfast, we took our walk, almost a sprint really, since we were keeping up with Theresa's chatting. Her date had been a home run, and she couldn't wait to talk about it. She had had her meeting with William Quinn, and it had been just as intense as mine, but her time with Michael more than made up for it.

"Should I spend time with him or wait for William?"

I considered her words. "You don't know if he'll find your soul mate. What can it hurt to spend time with Michael? He might even be the one for you."

She clutched my arm so tightly I thought she might leave bruises. "That's what I thought, too. How about you? I saw you had a dinner date. He looked so handsome."

I wrinkled my nose. "Not a date so much as a reunion. I dated Jaxon in high school. It was more of a closure kind of thing. Now I'm ready to move on."

Theresa gave me a quizzical glance, but I wasn't going to share any more. I was done talking about that. It was time for me to do what I'd said I was going to do: move on. "William Quinn texted me. He has someone for me to meet."

She clapped her hands, her eyes shining. "When are you meeting him? Can I come? I promise I'll lurk nearby and nothing more. I just want to see."

I'll admit, I was relieved to have someone there, someone on my side. "I would be thrilled to have you there. I'm nervous, actually. What if William is wrong?"

She cocked her head. "What if he's right?"

Oh God. What if he *was* right, and this guy was my soul mate? Was I really prepared for that?

The party on the town green was in full force by the time Theresa and I made our appearance. We toured the vendors' tents. I bought a few souvenirs to take back home. We listened to a local band on the stage in the center. And we sampled food and wine from local vineyards. I was feeling happy and relaxed, even as I kept looking around for Jaxon's familiar frame.

He had grown up, filled out his six foot two frame with muscle, and grown a dark brown, neatly trimmed beard that looked damned good on him. Not that I wanted to admit it. I hardened my resolve not to go back over the past even as I made sure he wasn't lurking around the festival grounds. But he wasn't around, not that I saw, and I grew tenser as the time came for me to meet my destiny. It didn't help that Theresa kept talking about how this was my future, and everything was going to change for me. No pressure or anything.

Finally, it was time. I left her by a fried dough stand with Michael, who had joined us and appeared to be just as besotted with her as she was with him. I made my way to the booth that was labeled *The Matchmaker* to see William Quinn standing inside with his granddaughter talking to a third person, in the shadows of the tent.

I paused and took a deep breath. It was time.

I walked to the tent, and William turned, his face wreathed

in smiles. "Sadie, dear. I'm so glad you could make it. I'd like you to meet your match."

He gestured to the figure who stepped out of the shadows, and my heart stopped.

Jaxon Bigsly.

CHAPTER SIX

JAXON

I cursed as Sadie whirled on her heel and bolted from the tent, but not before I saw the look of utter betrayal on her face. I pushed through Drew, Colleen, and William and followed her. I paused for a moment, searching the crowd for her honey-blond hair. She had been wearing it down, loose, and wavy around her shoulders and not in the ponytail that she often wore back in high school. My fingers itched to run through the strands, to see if they were as soft as they looked, as soft as I remembered. But I sensed that, especially now, she'd be even more unlikely to allow me to touch her, if she even let me speak to her after this fiasco.

Her words at dinner last night had almost gutted me, the finality of them a death knell on any lingering hope I had of winning her back. I had gotten my dinner to go and taken it back to my apartment, but I couldn't be bothered to eat, my appetite thoroughly gone after Sadie telling me goodbye. My business partner had called to complete our plans, and I'd almost pulled out. What was the point of returning to Holly Creek? My reason for going back, winning Sadie, was gone. But I had always wanted to run my own brewery, and we'd worked too hard for this opportunity. It was time to man up and deal with it.

Though after sandbagging her, she might actively try to sabotage me now.

I glimpsed honey-blond hair and a green sleeveless top. A flash of green and white skirt confirmed my quarry, and I beelined for the spot where I'd spied her, catching up rather quickly as Sadie power walked through the crowd, headed for the parking lot.

I grabbed her arm, and she came around swinging. I dropped her arm and ducked just in time. "Whoa, it's just me."

"Just the man I wanted to hit." She glared at me, tears shimmering in her eyes, belying the anger in her tone. "How could you, Jaxon?"

I held up my hands and took a step back. "It wasn't me. I swear. I didn't know this was why Drew texted. William apparently thought we were a match. I hadn't even applied to be set up."

She folded her arms in front of her, her jaw set in a mulish line, and stared at me, clearly not believing a word I said. We stood behind the vendor tents so the crowd was thinner back here, mostly support personnel and vendor staff who stared at us curiously, enough to make me herd her farther back toward the parking lot and away from prying eyes. I didn't need any more witnesses to my groveling.

She wrenched her arm out of my hold and backed away. "Stop manhandling me."

"Sorry. I just wanted fewer witnesses for our conversation."

"I would prefer none, if it were up to me." Her arms were folded again, her whole body closed as she hugged herself.

Damn it. Why had Drew and William done this to me? Had they known about our history? I didn't know how they could have, but if they did, how? Putting that aside, there was a glimmer of hope in this whole situation, something Sadie might not have considered.

"I didn't know this was what William had in mind, but you have to admit, it could be a good thing."

She went very still and arched an eyebrow. "How do you mean?"

Sensing I was walking on very thin ice, I chose my words carefully. "Well, William Quinn has never been wrong in his matches. If he thinks we're meant to be together, that we're soul mates, then maybe we should give it another try."

She stared at me for a long moment, her expression carefully blank to mask the hurt I could still see in her eyes, then she barked a laugh. "You've got to be kidding me. After all these years, after you left me, you think we should just try again because some matchmaker has decided that we're meant to be together?"

"I didn't just leave you, Sadie. I needed some time. I thought you understood that." I may not have handled our breakup eight years ago as well as I could have, but I didn't think it was that bad.

She took a step back, still hugging herself. "No, Jaxon. I don't think I'll ever really understand. But it's the past, and this is the present. Your matchmaker made a mistake. We may have once been a good match. But that was the past. I don't regret my life or my choices. I only regret coming here because it dangled a false hope in front of me."

She turned and fled into the mass of parked cars, leaving me behind. I sensed someone coming up next to me.

"Sorry if we blindsided you, man. Granddad said she was your perfect match," Drew said. "We didn't know you two had a history. What are you going to do now?"

"Is your granddad ever wrong?" I watched the Forester drive out of the parking lot and head out of town.

"Not that I know of. But he'll tell you it's complicated.

People might be soul mates, but they still have to want it to make a relationship work. It's not magic, not completely. The magic is only in the possibilities, opening your eyes to what could be. Then you need to do the hard stuff to make it a reality." He gave me a sideways look. "So what are you going to do?"

I had always known that Sadie and I had something special. I'd let my fears, my own issues, take me away, drive me to a future outside of Holly Creek. But now my path was leading me home, back to her. And I had a powerful incentive. Not just a business opportunity, but a matchmaker telling both of us that we were meant to be together.

"I'm going to win her back."

CHAPTER SEVEN

SADIE

The following Monday, I went into Choco Dee Lites early, hoping I could have a few hours of peace while I made some new candies for the summer tourist season. While spending time in Lovelorn had not resulted in my soul mate or even a date for Chelsea's wedding, I still had a few months to find one. I was sure that someone would appear. I had time, and online dating was still a thing, right?

What Lovelorn had given me was another avenue for my business. I had spoken with William Quinn's granddaughter, Colleen, about possibly being a vendor at their Valentine's Day event next year. She had loved my business and thought it would be an excellent addition to the smaller vendor group. She introduced me to one of the vineyard owners, and we discussed a chocolate and wine pairing experience to enhance the match-making atmosphere. Eden McIntyre was getting married later this year and was also interested in having my chocolates as party favors. I made a mental note to send Colleen and Eden samples for a tasting and get their thoughts on flavors for the events. So the trip to Lovelorn hadn't been a complete waste of time.

"At least you can write it off as a business expense," Clara declared from her perch on a high stool in the shop's kitchen as she waited to taste test the first piece of chocolate from the newest batch.

I had omitted the part where I had been matched to my high school boyfriend and the guy who'd broken my heart. I couldn't bring myself to go that far. Truth be told, I had gotten closure with Jaxon, and if we had left it at the dinner, it would have been fine. I didn't know who was to blame for the crossed wires on the matchmaking, but I could have done without that whole mess.

A knocking at my back door interrupted our conversation, and Clara jumped down to open it. Lila Addison had been a couple of years behind of me in school, and when she got married, she was my first customer for my chocolate. She was also my first employee until she produced two of the cutest rugrats around. Now she spent her time shuttling them to school and their forays into sporting events with her husband Tom and worked part-time with me a couple of times a week as needed.

She smiled when she saw me. "Perfect timing! Chocolate is just what the doctor ordered."

The doctor being her husband, of course, a general physician in town. She popped up on the stool next to Clara and snagged a piece of candy from the cooling rack. "Perfect, as usual. So how was the trip?"

I shot her a severe look, ignoring her innocent act. "You know exactly how it went. Don't lie to me, Lila Bigsly Addison."

Clara's eyes widened, and Lila's gaze slid away. She chewed on her lower lip. "I can explain, really, Sadie."

I folded my hands in front of me and arched my eyebrow at her. "Oh, really? I can't wait to hear this one."

I had chewed on this the whole drive back from Lovelorn. How could Lila have let me go to Lovelorn knowing her brother was there, knowing our history? Because there was no way that she hadn't known her brother had been living there for the past couple of years. A little warning would have been nice. Judging by the guilt on her face, she knew and had been playing a little matchmaking of her own.

"I wasn't sure you'd even see him. He's been busy with his brewery."

I gave her a look that let her know exactly what I thought of that lame excuse. Clara, though, was fairly bouncing on her stool. "Hello? A little context for the third person in the room. What happened?"

With an apologetic glance at me, Lila turned to Clara. "My brother, Jaxon, has been living in Lovelorn. She apparently ran into him there this past week."

I braced my hands on the counter and leaned forward. "I didn't just run into him. That damned matchmaker matched us."

Clara's jaw dropped, and Lila's face widened in a big smile. "I knew it! You two were always meant to be together." She hopped off the stool and did her own uncoordinated version of a victory dance, complete with hands waving in the air and stomping feet. "I always knew the two of you should end up together, and now we have confirmation."

I wrapped my arms around myself again, refusing to agree. I had been there, done that before. I wasn't sure I could trust him not to leave again. Not that it mattered. I wasn't interested in a long-distance romance. I just needed a date for the wedding. I could deal with long-term later.

"Well, it doesn't matter, anyway. He's in Lovelorn and I'm in Holly Creek. So I need to find someone closer, at least within an hour's driving distance. For now, I want to focus on the business. Lovelorn brought me some new business opportunities."

Lila went back to chewing on her lower lip and avoiding my gaze. A suspicious feeling grew in my stomach. Before I could say anything, Clara glanced at Lila. "Did you say his name was Jaxon? Jaxon Bigsly?"

Lila nodded, still not meeting my gaze, and that feeling grew, almost like the time I had food poisoning and I was on a deserted road with nowhere to stop.

"Isn't he the guy who just bought Tap Meister Brewery?"

I froze and slowly pivoted to spear my employee and former best friend with a deadly look. Both women avoided my gaze like champions. "Lila. Clara. Did Jaxon Bigsly just buy Tap Meister Brewery?"

They exchanged uneasy glances, which only confirmed my worst fear. Then Lila looked at me, apprehension in every tense line of her face. "Yes, he did, with his partner, Sean Wallace."

I closed my eyes and took a deep breath, counting to ten, then twenty, then on to fifty, because I needed the time. Why the hell hadn't Jaxon mentioned it when I was in Lovelorn? He had plenty of time to tell me he was moving back to Holly Creek. Better yet, why hadn't my best friend, or former best friend, his own sister, not told me about this? Instead, she'd let me be blindsided twice by the ex who'd destroyed me.

"How could you not tell me, Lila?"

Guilt riddled her face, and she sagged on the stool, her hands buried in her lap. "I wanted to tell you, but Jax asked me to keep it quiet since the owner was being difficult about selling. In fact, he wasn't sure if Jed would even sell for a while."

I rolled my eyes. We all knew Tap Meister had been in trouble. Jed Turner's son wanted nothing to do with it, preferring his life in New York City, and the brewery had been in decline for a few years. The best we could all hope for was new owners who would bring new life to it, along with tourists for tastings and job opportunities. But Jed was notoriously cranky and difficult to deal with, being stubborn about deciding anything. The business side of me should be happy that we had a sale, as it would help bring new tourists into the town, but the woman in me hated that it was Jaxon. Dare I hope he would be an absentee owner?

"Is he at least staying in Lovelorn with his job there?"

Lila wouldn't meet my eyes, but she shook her head. Of course not. Why would he stay as a brew master for another brewery when he could run his own? Even I knew that was a stupid question. If only Holly Creek was bigger, so I wouldn't have to see him, but we were only about four thousand people now. And knowing my luck, I'd run into Jaxon every other day, never mind at the Chamber of Commerce meetings every couple of months. Maybe it was time to find a new site for my business.

Lila glanced at her watch and squealed. "I have to run and pick up the kids. Just think about it, Sadie. Give him a chance." She hugged me and ran out the door in a flurry of activity, leaving Clara and me alone.

I went back to fiddling with the display, even though it was just fine. Clara continued to study me with her shrewd eyes, not fooled at all. Finally, I straightened. "Okay, let me know what you think."

Clara pursed her lips thoughtfully. "I didn't know you and Jaxon back then. I only moved here a few years ago and heard about the golden couple and how perfect you were. But that was high school. Nothing is ever perfect in high school, even if we think they are."

"Lila and Tom are." I couldn't keep the bitterness out of my voice.

"Lila and Tom are a freak of nature," Clara retorted good-naturedly. "And didn't they only start dating after high school, when he came back during college? So you see, they were not a high school romance. We see life different when we're teenagers. Lord knows I made a ton of mistakes."

My heart stuttered. "Jaxon and I weren't a mistake."

Clara's voice gentled. "I'm not saying you were. I'm just

saying that maybe it wasn't your time. You both needed to grow into who you were meant to be."

I pondered her words. Maybe we weren't meant to be together. Maybe our breakup was a good thing. I don't regret going to culinary school and opening my shop. Could I have done that if I had gotten married and had kids right away? Or would I have followed Jaxon as he took jobs at various breweries? I definitely wouldn't have my shop then. Maybe it was for the best that we broke up. It was hard to give up on that idea of who we had once been, especially when I was constantly reminded of it.

"Maybe you're right. Maybe we weren't meant to be together. I just find it hard to understand that he never wanted to live in Holly Creek and now he's back. Why is he back here?"

Clara cocked her head. "Maybe he's seen the world and is ready to settle down. Maybe he wants you back. Don't let your hurt over the past hold you back from what you could have now."

I shook my head. "Nope, we had our come to Jesus and we're done. Kaput. Over. That ship has sailed."

Clara eyed me shrewdly. "Well, if it's over, then why is it bothering you so much? I never said you weren't meant to be. I only said it wasn't the right time. Maybe you are meant to be, and the timing is finally right. Could now be the right time?"

CHAPTER EIGHT

JAXON

I stood alone in the wooden brew pub portion of Tap Meister, fingering the ring of keys dangling from my hand. The space had been left exactly as the previous owner had it, since Sean and I had bought it lock, stock, and barrel. On the surface, the brew pub room was updated, with exposed wooden beams, windows to the brewing areas to allow the patrons to feel a part of the process, and the bare rustic elements giving off a rough, woodsy feel. At least old Jed Turner had kept up this part of the place. But this was where his money had come from, where he hosted events in the small town of Holly Creek.

There weren't a lot of other options for people to have big events in town, unless you wanted to use the church basement, which was a choice for some people. But this place was all mine now—well, mine and Sean's. Now I could update it and the parts no one saw, like the equipment and the beer that we made to bring Tap Meister into the twenty-first century, with updated ales and lagers and brews, expanding our distributions and growing our business. It was so exciting. My fingers itched to dive into the bag and check on my most recent brew.

My cell rang, and I laughed. "Hey, Sean. Where the hell are you?"

"I'm at the bank, wrapping up some paperwork. It's ours. Everything is signed, sealed and delivered." My partner's voice came over the speakerphone, echoing in the space.

"Yup. I just finished the walkthrough. Fortunately, everything came through without a hitch."

"Old Jed didn't pull any last-minute bullshit?"

It was a fair question. Jed had been dancing around us like a prize fighter working on his heavyweight boxing championship belt and floating around more than Muhammed Ali. But we'd finally pinned him down when it appeared his creditors were circling like vultures, though he swore he had the honey for bees. Either way, we gave him a way out and a place to come to every day if he wanted to still be involved in operations. Sean had been in and out of the area over the past couple of months, working the financial details and making a plan for distributors and buyers he hoped to meet with, but I had to do the final walkthrough of the brewery to ensure everything was all set on site.

I remembered coming to work here with my father when I was in elementary school. I thought this was the most exciting place ever and used to sit with old Jed or follow him around, as the old man taught me all about the beer he was making, while my father worked various jobs in the brewery. My father had long since stopped working there, but I never lost my fondness for the place or for beer. When I went to college and, like other frat guys, sitting around drinking beer and joking about opening a pub or a brewery, I met Sean and we discovered we were serious about our plans. Once we realized each of us had skills to help each other—Sean as a small business consultant and me as a brew master—we teamed up and made our plans.

Now we had achieved it. Phase one complete. On to phase two. "Nope, I think he was relieved, even if he wouldn't admit it."

Sean snorted. "Sure he was. Have you seen his debt? Our buyout was extremely generous. We could have saved ourselves money, you know."

"I couldn't do that to him, Sean. Besides, Holly Creek is a small town. Word would get around, and people wouldn't be happy if we screwed Jed."

"We didn't screw him. He did it to himself. This was business." A familiar refrain from my friend and partner, but I knew he wasn't really upset. He understood the situation. "So you're settled? How is the beer?"

That had been the first thing I'd checked. I had a recipe I was planning for Oktoberfest and had convinced Jed to let us start brewing it early, as we were working through the sale. It was a risk, but I'd played on Jed's connection with me from the past. Well, that and a little strong-arming. The beer had brewed and was fermenting now, almost ready for bottling. We were on track as planned.

"It's in the fermenting tanks. We're on track to bottle next week."

"Good deal. Load me up with samples as soon as you can. I've got a couple of consulting jobs still to wrap up over the coming weeks, but in between, every minute will be about us. Beer won't sell itself."

I chuckled softly. I did appreciate his drive to get the job done. He would have our distribution lined up in no time.

"And Sadie?" How is she?"

My chuckling died at Sean's words. He had brought up the one fly in the ointment. I hadn't mentioned that I had seen her the previous week, and she had been very clear that we were over. I hadn't seen her since coming back to town, since I had only gotten in last night. But she was next on my list before someone else told her.

My phone beeped, and I saw my sister's name. "Hold that thought. My sister's calling."

"Say hi for me. I should be there as soon as I finish here at the bank."

I switched over the call to my sister, who, as usual, didn't bother with a hello. "Not even in town twenty-four hours and you already fucked up with Sadie? That's a new record, even for you."

Shit. "She knows?"

"Oh yeah, she knows. And she's not happy. Well, that's an understatement. What happened in Lovelorn?"

I quickly outlined the conversation, and Lila was silent on the other end of the phone for so long, I wondered if we'd been disconnected. "Okay, you're a dumbass. You should have stayed away, but you didn't. Now she thinks you lied to her for years and didn't care enough to see her when you were only a couple of hours away."

"You didn't tell her either," I couldn't help but point out, knowing it was petty and probably made me a jerk, but whatever.

"Yeah, but I'm her best friend, not her ex-boyfriend who destroyed her when he left. She'll forgive me, eventually. She has a voodoo doll of you that she sticks pins in when she is feeling particularly pissed off. I'd lie low for a few days until she cools off. Then we'll regroup."

A shadow moved outside the door to the brewery and it opened, then slammed shut behind a woman. "Too late. She's here."

"Oh. You are so fucked. Have a nice day!" Lila ended the call.

Sadie stormed into the taproom at Tap Meister, all fury and beauty. I had forgotten how beautiful she was when she was mad. Though, when we were dating, she had rarely ever been angry with me. I'm sure she had been furious when I broke things off, but I had taken the chickenshit way out and did it over the phone, telling her that I wasn't coming back after college. I needed to spread my wings beyond our small town of Holly Creek.

Okay, I lied, and someday I would have to tell her the truth about why I'd really left, but how could I admit the truth? And if I did, would I lose any remaining emotion she had for me? Granted, the only emotion she had right now was anger, and I had to hope that the old adage was true. You only got angry when you cared for someone.

Sadie stalked across the space until she stood right in front of me. "You couldn't have mentioned this a few days ago when I saw you in Lovelorn? I'm sure this didn't just happen overnight."

I put my hands up, hoping it would calm her down. "Sadie, I didn't want to spoil the surprise. Besides, I had just found out and didn't want to jinx it."

She cocked her head and narrowed her gaze at me, clearly not buying what I was selling. "Bull. You don't just finalize the sale on a business in three days. This has been in the works for a while. Why didn't you warn me?"

I folded my arms in front of me and leaned against the tall counter, the very image of a casual business owner when the last thing I felt was relaxed. "Honestly, I didn't think you'd care. Based on the way we left things, you were over me and our relationship, so this shouldn't matter. Was that wrong?"

She stared at me, her hazel eyes snapping with frustration. "You know it wasn't. But I didn't think I'd see you again."

She was magnificent, and I doubted she wanted me to tell her how fucking sexy she looked right now and how much she was turning me on. I settled for tucking a strand of her honey blond hair that had come loose from her bun behind her ear since I doubted she would let me kiss her. "And now?"

"I should think that should be obvious. I'm furious that you didn't tell me. How could you?"

The hurt in her voice almost gutted me. I had done that to her, and no amount of restitution now would ease it. I only hoped with time Sadie would forgive me and we could move forward. "I had planned on going to your shop as soon as I had signed the papers and completed the walkthrough. I literally just finished all of that. How did you find out so fast?"

"Your sister and Clara, my assistant. They were only too happy to share the news."

I cursed under my breath. Lila could have warned me before throwing me under the bus. "I'm sorry. I wanted to be the one to tell you. But now that you know, is this going to be a problem?"

She wrapped her arms around her waist, a protective gesture that wasn't lost on me. "I guess it depends on why you're really here. Is it just for the brewery?"

I gentled my tone, easing her into my real purpose. "I thought it would have been obvious. Sure, I want to renovate Tap Meister. I've always loved it. But you're right. I have another goal." My eyes met hers, trying to show my determination and love for her.

"I'm here to win you back."

CHAPTER NINE

SADIE

*J*axon's familiar blue eyes met mine, filled with determination and an emotion I never thought I'd see again. "I'm here to win you back."

I swallowed hard, my mind racing as I tried to process his words. The warmth of the sun streaming through the windows seemed to pale compared to the heat that radiated from Jaxon, igniting a fire within me that I thought had long been extinguished. I had been such a fool to think that I was over Jaxon Bigsly. Clara was so right. I couldn't outrun our history.

"Win me back?" I scoffed, feigning indifference while my heart threatened to burst from my ribcage. "That's quite the assumption, Jaxon."

His gaze never faltered as he took a step closer, closing the distance between us. "It's not an assumption, Sadie. It's a fact. I know I messed up before, but I've changed. I just need a chance to prove it to you."

"Changed?" My eyes narrowed, searching for any sign of insincerity. "Prove it how? By buying a brewery and turning it into some... trendy hotspot?"

"By showing you that I'm serious about my future. Our

future." His voice was thick with emotion, his eyes pleading with me to believe him.

The familiar ache spread deep in my chest as I weighed the sincerity of his words against the pain of our past. A war waged within me—one side desperate for the love I had once known and the other determined to protect myself against the pain that I was afraid to feel again. But as Jaxon reached out to brush a stray lock of hair from my face again, the warmth of his touch sent shivers down my spine, leaving me questioning if I could ever truly let go of the man who had once held my heart so completely.

"Jaxon," I whispered, my resolve wavering under the weight of his unwavering gaze, "I... I don't know if I can do this again."

"Trust me, Sadie," he murmured, his fingers lingering on my cheek, igniting a spark that threatened to consume us both. "I won't let you down this time."

I felt the warmth of his touch, my heart pounding in my chest as I struggled to maintain my composure. The morning sun cast a soft golden glow on his rugged features, accentuating every line and curve that had once been so achingly familiar. My breath hitched as I took in his once familiar face, the boy I once knew now grown into the man before me, and I wondered if I could risk my heart again or if it was too late and I was already lost.

"Jaxon," I began, the words heavy with emotion, "I appreciate your honesty and... and everything you've said. But things have changed. I've moved on."

His blue eyes clouded with confusion, and for a moment, he seemed at a loss for words. His hand dropped from my cheek, leaving an empty space where his warmth had once lingered.

"Moved on?" he echoed, disbelief lacing his voice. "Sadie, I know we've both made mistakes, but don't you think we owe it to ourselves to try again?"

The memory of our past weighed heavily on my heart. I

couldn't help but recall the countless nights I'd spent crying myself to sleep, wondering what I could have done differently. I shook my head, fighting back the tears that threatened to spill over.

"I can't go through that again. I've built a life for myself here in Holly Creek. A life that doesn't include you."

"Sadie, please," he implored, desperation etched across his face. "I'm not asking you to throw away everything you've worked for. I just want a chance to show you that I've changed. That we can be better together than we were apart."

My chest tightened at the sincerity in his voice, and for a fleeting moment, I allowed herself to imagine a future with Jaxon by my side—the laughter we would share, the love that would endure even the most trying of times. But my heart couldn't ignore the uncertainty that whispered in the back of my mind, a constant reminder of the pain he'd caused when he walked away.

"I can't," I whispered, my voice barely audible over the sound of the brewery's doors creaking in the distance, and the faint smell of hops and barley wafting through the air.

"I'll do whatever it takes," he pleaded. "Please, just give me another chance."

As I stared into the depths of his ocean-blue eyes, I knew that despite the love that still lingered between us, there was no going back. I had come too far to risk losing myself again. I shook my head, my fists clenched at my side.

"No, Jaxon," I whispered, the words laced with finality. "We've both changed, grown into different people. What we had... it was great, but it's over now."

His jaw clenched, and I could see the storm raging within him - hurt, anger, disbelief. "Is this what you truly want?" he asked, his voice strained, as if each word was a battle. "To walk away from us, without even considering what we could become?"

"Sometimes," I replied, tears blurring my vision, "the hardest choices are the ones that set us free."

"Damn it, Sadie!" Jaxon exclaimed, running a hand through his sandy blond hair in frustration. "Why are you so afraid of taking a chance on us? We were great together, and we could be even better now. Just give me a chance to prove it to you."

I swallowed hard, feeling the weight of our history pressing down on me. "You're right. We were great once. But that was then. This is now. And I can't keep living in the past, hoping for something that may never be."

He took a step toward me, his blue eyes pleading with me to reconsider. "I'm not asking you to live in the past, Sadie. I'm asking you to let me in, to let me show you how much I love you. To let us have a future. Is that really so terrifying?"

"Or maybe," Jaxon continued, his voice low and intense, "you're afraid of the love we could have—a love that could set us both free."

My breath caught in my throat at his words, the truth of them ringing like a bell within me. But I couldn't allow myself to be swayed, not when my heart was at stake. "I just... can't."

"Fine," he said finally, his jaw set in determination. "If you won't give us a chance, then I guess there's nothing left for me to do but fight for you—and for the love I know we can have."

With those words, he strode away, disappearing into the back area of the brewery, leaving me standing alone in the taproom. I watched him go, my heart aching with a mixture of fear and hope. This wasn't over. He wasn't going to just walk away. I had to be strong. I couldn't risk my heart and wait for him to walk away again.

JAXON

I drove down the narrow streets of my childhood neighborhood, past Old Lady Wharton's house who used to give out full-sized candy bars at Halloween. Past the empty place where the old oak tree was that we took turns climbing and where I fell and broke my arm when I was eight. Dad was so pissed at me for blowing an entire season of peewee football that year. Then past the Taylor house, the arts and crafts-style home that looked just as warm and inviting as it always had. My eyes immediately went to the second-floor window where Sadie slept and the tree outside her window. I got really good at climbing trees after I broke my arm. Of course, with Sadie as a motivation, I'd climb all day to get to her window.

But the lights were off in the old bedroom. I was sure she didn't live here anymore. My sister had told me that Sadie rented part of a two-family house closer to her store. She wanted a house, but she didn't have time for the yard work, not with the business. That was a damned shame. Sadie loved gardening, though maybe she had a small flower garden at her place. Not that she'd invite me to see it anytime soon.

I continued past the Taylor house. They weren't my target. I had bigger ghosts to deal with. A few houses down, I pulled in to a single-story brick ranch house that had seen better days. It was summer, but the grass was burned, and what wasn't yellow from the summer sun was filled with crabgrass and assorted weeds. The box bushes that lined the front of the house hadn't been trimmed that year, and stone had replaced the mulch that used to surround the bushes. The mountain laurel by the front door was overgrown and overshadowed the front walkway and the two steps to the front door.

I sighed. I should have come home sooner to help my father. My sister's husband tried to help where he could, but he had his own place, plus the kids. Also, Dad could be a real pain in the ass, which didn't make things any easier. Now I was home, and I had more amends to make to more people than just Sadie. Hopefully, this one would be easier.

I pulled into the driveway behind Lila's car. She must have rushed over here to ease my way with Dad. She had a way with him, as daughters did with their fathers, whereas sons and their dads often clashed like brawlers in a prize fight.

Lila came down the walkway and waited for me to get out of the car. For an insane moment, I thought about backing out and driving away. But I was done running. Everything I wanted was within reach. The brewery. Sadie. My future. I just had to do the fucking work.

I barely got out of the car when Lila rushed me, hugging me so tightly I was afraid she'd cut off my air. But I hugged her back just as tightly. It was good to be home. "Ease up, little sister. Don't kill me before Dad has a chance."

She pulled back and whacked me on the arm with a fist. "That's for Sadie, though I'm sure she can handle herself just fine."

I winced and rubbed my arm, though thinking about how I had left things with Sadie and the sadness in her still gutted me.

"She's pretty pissed off and wants nothing to do with me," I admitted.

Lila folded her arms in front of her and arched her eyebrow. "Do you blame her? You bailed on her with barely an explanation, which was a dick move, then you move a couple of hours away and never told her."

"You didn't tell her either," I reminded her yet again.

"Yeah, but I'm the friend who bashes you with her every girls' night. You're the one who broke her heart. What's the plan, brother? You going to stick around or head out when the going gets tough?"

"Depends. How tough will it get?" I joked, then I sobered at her arch look. "Seriously, I'm staying. I bought a business, Lila. Why would I leave?"

"You could always hire people to run it for you or sell it. You're going to have to do the work, Jax. And it won't be easy. Not with some people."

I sighed, knowing she was right. So I changed the subject, though not by much. "How is he?"

She glanced over her shoulder at the curtains in the front picture window that twitched shut. "You know, sunshine, puppies, and unicorn farts."

"That good, huh? Thanks for taking care of him all these years. I know it can't have been easy, especially after the accident." I tugged her close and hugged her again, giving her a noogie.

She shrieked and ducked away, laughing. "Come on. I made dinner for all of us. Try not to start anything until after we've all eaten."

Remembering Thanksgiving and Dad passed out drunk on the couch before dinner ended, I shuddered. "I'll do my best, Lila."

✳

*W*e made it through dinner with only minimal scarring. Dad had to put his two cents in through the entire meal, digs about me not playing football in college, not living up to my potential, and the opening for a football coach at the high school. Like I wanted to revisit my glory days. I think he had conveniently forgotten that I had blown out my shoulder freshman year at Syracuse University during training camp and never went back, not that I was ever slated to be anything more than a backup to the first-string players.

While Dad went back for his fourth beer, I wandered outside in the backyard where a new play set had been put up for Lila and Tom's kids. They were already scrambling on the set. Six-year-old Caleb was swinging, kicking off to get as high as he could, and four-year-old Ella was sliding down the little slide and scrambling back up. I leaned against the old picnic table and watched them for a few minutes.

Tom came out the sliding glass door and dropped a beer on the table. "Last year's batch. I can't wait to see what you'll do with Tap Meister and the new brews you'll come up with."

"If I listen to Dad, I'm just deluding myself, thinking I could do anything good with Tap Meister." I heard the tone of bitterness in my voice but didn't bother to stop it. Tom had been a classmate of mine, and we'd been on the football team together throughout school. I couldn't be happier for him and Lila, once I got past the thought of my sister with a friend.

He shrugged. "Your dad has issues. You know that, Jax."

I rolled my eyes. "You don't say. Could it be that I never went pro with football? Never was on television playing college ball? There is more to life than football. You'd think we lived in the South or Texas the way that man worships the sport."

"He doesn't worship football. He just thought it was your ticket to something better. A better life, more money, whatever.

Hell, I think we all thought you had that chance. We had never come close to state champs before or after you. That year was pure magic, Jax. You brought it, led us all the way. It wasn't hard to imagine you going further."

I snorted and took a deep swallow of the beer. Yeah, mine was going to be so much better than this, though it wasn't half bad. "I was a big fish in a little pond. Trust me when I say there were plenty of fish out there, and I wasn't so big when it came down to it."

"Is that what happened? Did you decide you weren't big enough?" Tom asked quietly.

I considered his question for a moment, then shook my head. "No, I never wanted to play football forever, believe it or not. It wasn't my dream. It was always Dad's dream. He was the king of his team, so he made me into a mini-me, only I was supposed to go further. I just didn't have the skills or the desire."

Ella fell off the slide and cried. Tom hurried over and soothed her for a few moments. After a brief cuddle with her dad, she wiggled out of his arms and was back to climbing up the slide while her brother continued to shoot for the sky. Tom ambled back over and sat across from me.

"What about Sadie?"

I grimaced. "Did Lila send you out here to pump me for information?"

He grinned. "Happy wife, happy life. I live to please that woman."

I grinned back. "Damn right you do, or I'll kick your ass."

He smirked. "You can try. But seriously, you left, and now you're back. Everyone thought you guys were *the couple*. What happened?"

I tipped the bottle back and stared at my niece and nephew playing. If I had made different choices, they could have been my kids. I could have had everything, including Tap Meister, if I had only stayed here in town. I could have apprenticed to Jed, worked at the brewery, married Sadie, and never left Holly Creek.

Now what did I have? No wife, just the brewery. But I had no regrets, well, except for how I'd left things with Sadie. I'd needed to leave, to spread my wings, to learn things and meet people I would never have met if I'd stayed here.

"Do you regret staying?"

"And marrying Lila? Nope. I'm happy right here. I'm a doctor, helping my community, and am raising two wonderful children, all in my hometown with my family nearby. What's not to love?" He looked at me. "No one blames you for leaving. Everyone has to make their own choices. Hell, half our high school graduating class bolted as soon as they could. Don't worry about it."

"And Sadie?"

Tom grimaced. "Yeah, you're on your own with that one. My wife will have something to say about that." He stood and put the bottle on the table. "Oh, and one more thing. If you ever disappear again and decide not to come back and visit often, I've been tasked with kicking your ass. Just a warning."

I laughed. "Bring it."

But I had no intention of leaving Holly Creek. Not anymore. I was home to stay.

CHAPTER ELEVEN

SADIE

Oktoberfest. While it wasn't the biggest festival in Holly Creek, it did kick off our town's festival season. Holly Creek was known mostly for our Christmas displays and events, but we started with Oktoberfest to bring in the leaf peepers and fall lovers from the city and the surrounding areas. Holly Creek was gorgeous in the autumn, another reason I never wanted to leave.

I always had a special display for Oktoberfest, as did most of the shop owners, to lure tourists into our shops, while some had booths on the town green around the Biergarten. Fall and Christmas helped us make our profits for the year. A low turnout could spell disaster for some of the smaller businesses. Since Tap Meister had been slowing down production over the past several years, Oktoberfest hadn't been the same. Sure, we'd supplemented with other fall festivities, but everyone knew Oktoberfest wasn't complete without a kick-ass Biergarten, with special beers only available at the festival. It had been many years since there had been a special beer for Oktoberfest. It was doubtful that this year would be any different.

I sat in the third row in the basement of the town hall

listening to our mayor, Ezekiel Barrett, and the members of the town council talk about various matters regarding the town. The festival, and all other events, were slated to be covered last. I clutched my notebook and folders with my papers tighter, my knuckles turning white as the council droned on about new crosswalks or something. It was important, but I tuned them out as I ran through my agenda again in my head.

A shape slid into the metal folding chair next to me, jostling me out of my thoughts. "What did I miss?"

I stiffened as the familiar voice and scent washed over me. Jaxon. Without even turning, I spoke out of the side of my mouth. "There are over a dozen other seats in the room. Pick one of them."

He stared at me. "I did. This one was close to the front, and you know how I like to hear everything that's going on."

I shifted so I was facing him. "No, you sat in the back with the other football players and relied on my notes for studying. When you actually studied."

He gave me his charming, megawatt smile that probably still had ladies dropping their panties everywhere, especially in a town like Lovelorn that had women flocking there looking for their one true love. "You still mad because I didn't study as much as you yet still made the National Honor Society? It's because I listened to everything you said when we studied together. I learned from you. Honestly, I thought you would have been a teacher since you were so good at teaching me."

I snorted, and the people in front of us turned and glared. Old Mrs. Hubbard from the floral shop shushed me, and I apologized while Jaxon gave her a smile. She fluttered her eyelashes and blushed, then gave me a nasty look and turned around.

I huffed my annoyance. "That old bat. I buy a bouquet from her every week, and she gives me the stink eye while you just have to smile and she melts at your feet."

Jaxon stretched out his legs and dropped an arm on the chair behind me. "I have a way with the ladies."

I shot him a sour look. "Yeah, I'm aware."

He straightened. "I never cheated, Sadie. That wasn't why I left."

Dammit. I knew that. That was what made the breakup so hard. If he had cheated or wanted to date someone else, I could make him out to be a bad guy, more than I already did, but he just wanted his freedom away from me. "Yeah, I know Jaxon. You just didn't want me."

He opened his mouth to reply, and before he could speak, Zeke spoke from the front. "Sadie? Are you ready to update us on your Oktoberfest plans?"

I sucked in a breath, striving for the calm that Jaxon had disturbed. I stood and walked to the podium placed in the center aisle. I spread out my papers and began my update. "The shop owners are all lined up for their vendor booths, along with several others from previous years. The food is also in place. I have a handout that itemizes all the details for you, including a list of the vendors and food suppliers. We have multiple entertainers lined up for Friday through Sunday, including music and comedians. We have some family-friendly options for the kids to enjoy and a variety of musical options from country to rock. I think it should appeal to everyone."

I handed the copies to Councilor Bush, and she passed them down to all the members of the Council. They bent their heads and studied the numbers. Zeke's eyes narrowed.

"This all looks excellent, Sadie, as usual. However, we appear to have one outstanding question. A big one. The Biergarten. Who will be running it?"

Damn. I had hoped to have a solution before tonight, or at least speak with Zeke privately before we had to make this decision, but clearly that wasn't going to happen. I took a deep breath and dove straight into the lion's den. "I had spoken with

Jed Turner a few weeks ago after he had ducked my calls for weeks. Of course, now we know why. He was selling Tap Meister. Finally, he told me that he couldn't sponsor the Biergarten this year. So we'll need another vendor. I was in Lovelorn a week or so ago and I checked on some possible sponsors. If you flip the page, you can see the options."

"Excuse me." Jaxon's voice rang out in the basement, and everyone turned. I cringed at his expression.

He strode up next to me, crowding me at the podium. "Some of you know me. Jaxon Bigsly. I just took over Tap Meister brewery with my partner. I'd like to know why we weren't considered for this."

Shit, he looked pissed.

CHAPTER TWELVE

JAXON

I couldn't believe what I was hearing. Was Sadie so pissed at me that she would block me from participating in the festival? I had purposely come to the meeting intending to volunteer the brewery, as it had run the Biergarten every year since I could remember. To be cut out like this was infuriating, especially when I was launching a new business. Was she that angry over our breakup?

Sadie slowly turned to face me, confusion written all over her face. "Jaxon, I didn't even know you owned Tap Meister. Jed told us that he couldn't sponsor the Biergarten this year and that was it. So I made alternate arrangements. Your actual issue is with him."

Oh, I definitely would speak to him, but that wasn't all. "You could have checked in with me before tonight, to confirm the situation with me."

Her face flushed, and she glanced away as my words found their target. Murmuring spread through the basement as people muttered among themselves. I ignored them and focused on the one woman who was the most important person in the room.

"Jaxon Bigsly, welcome back to Holly Creek. We're so glad

you're home." Zeke Bartlett rose to his feet, a big smile on his face.

Zeke had always been a big supporter of the Holly Creek high school football team, sponsoring us from his car dealership and even working in the concession stand. I'd bought my first car from him, a used Subaru with a decent amount of miles, but in great condition. That car carried me through quite a few years as I built my reputation and job history, moving around from internship to internship at various breweries.

Mrs. Hubbard stared up at me from her seat. "Does this mean you'll sponsor the Biergarten this year?"

Considering it had been one of our biggest marketing targets for the year and I had busted my ass working on a new brew for it, she could bet her ass I was sponsoring the Biergarten. Of course, that was assuming Sadie hadn't negotiated with anyone else to take our spot. Damn it, that Lovelorn trip had bitten me in the ass in more ways than one.

Instead of giving a smart-ass response, I turned to Mrs. Hubbard and the rest of the committee, putting on my most charming smile and avoiding looking at Sadie. I'd deal with her later. "Absolutely. As a vital member of the community, we at Tap Meister would be honored to support the town and the Biergarten. After all, it's tradition, isn't it?"

Sadie made a noise next to me that sounded surprisingly like a muttered, "Bullshit."

I turned my smile on her, but my eyes promised vengeance. "I'm sorry, Sadie. Is everything okay? Do you not want to support local business?"

Her eyes flashed fire, and I swore I could hear her teeth grinding, but she also bared her teeth in a facsimile of a smile. "Of course we want to support our businesses. But I wouldn't want to pressure you when you're new to opening your business. I know how much pressure can be on new owners."

The last was said with a sweet smile, but I didn't miss the

tiny barb hidden within. "We already planned for it. Of course, we'll have our grand opening Labor Day weekend first, so we'll be ready for the festival."

Zeke pounded his gavel. "Then it's settled. Sounds like the Oktoberfest is in excellent hands. Since Jaxon is newly returned and just taking over the brewery, he may want to work closely with Sadie to ensure the plans for the Biergarten are well in hand. We'll see you both in a couple of weeks for our next meeting and a status update. Meeting adjourned."

Sadie tried to interrupt, even raised her hand, bless her rule-following heart, but everyone ignored her. The meeting ended, and everyone broke off into smaller groups to catch up. Sadie started to duck out, but I wouldn't allow that. I tucked her elbow in my hand and hustled her over to the side.

She struggled a little, and when we got to the side, she wrenched free, glaring at me. "You could have just asked."

I snorted. "Like you would have come over here voluntarily?" She looked away, color staining her cheeks. "I thought so. I can't believe you hate me so much that you would sabotage my business."

Her head whipped up, and she stared at me in shock. "Jaxon, I never intended for that to happen. Seriously, I spoke to Jed, and he said he couldn't sponsor it."

"And you never thought to ask me, the new owner, once in the past few days?"

She opened and closed her mouth a couple of times, but before she could reply, a voice interrupted. "So it's true. The golden boy is back in Holly Creek. I never thought I'd see you back again."

I turned to see Devon Paxton, one of the council members and my old football teammate, standing a few feet away. Devon had not aged well, though that could be the sneer and the lines that proved his face wore that expression more often than an affable one. His blond hair was slicked back from his face and appeared to be thinning. The muscle from his football days as a middle linebacker had softened and settled from years of inactivity into huskiness. He wore a bespoke suit that did its best to hide the extra weight and reflect his status as council member and successful businessman. An overall image of a pillar of the community, while I was lucky that my worn jeans and flannel shirt were clean, considering I had been wrestling with a broken-down bottling machine before I realized I was late for the meeting. Judging by Devon's sneer, he wasn't impressed by me or my workman attire. I didn't know how I would survive the disappointment.

"Paxton. Long time no see." I refused to say that it was nice to see him or any such bullshit. We'd hated each other throughout school, and neither distance nor time had changed that.

My former nemesis seemed to have the same attitude since he never said he was glad I was back in town or that he'd missed me, either. "When I heard you wanted to buy Tap Meister, I have to admit I was surprised, especially with your father's... problem."

Red clouded my vision, and I clenched my fists at my sides. A hand landed on my forearm gently. "Devon, did you need something?"

Sadie's cool, soft voice interrupted, smoothing over the rough edges as she so often had throughout high school. Devon's gaze laser-focused on her, and I could almost imagine him panting after her as he had during school. While I was away, I dreaded hearing about the day Sadie dated Devon. He would never leave Holly Creek. He'd had a business handed to him and could be the big fish in the small pond, and he'd reveled in it, wanting nothing else. He would have been the perfect guy for her, the kind of guy who would stay here forever, except for the fact that he was a total douche. But there weren't a lot of options, and I worried she would eventually cave and become Mrs. Devon Paxton.

That would kill me. Anyone but Paxton.

Devon's greedy eyes ran over Sadie's black and white polka dot skirt and her black cardigan that fitted her perfectly, showing off her sexy figure. Sadie's shoulders hunched a little, but she stared at him coolly.

He licked his lips, attention focused on her breasts. I could understand it. They were magnificent, but he didn't have that right. "I was wondering if you'd like to go to the reunion with me."

The reunion? Oh shit. Our ten-year high school reunion was this year. I couldn't remember if I'd RSVP'd, but I was sure my sister had done it for me, since her husband was in my class and they were going. Damn it.

"Sorry, Paxton. I'm afraid I already have a date," I drawled, deliberately misunderstanding the man and lying at the same time. I was damn well going to have a date for it. In fact...I draped an arm across Sadie's shoulders, who froze like a rabbit scenting a hound dog.

Paxton also froze, his eyes narrowing to tiny little slits. Two spots of color rose in his cheeks, and his jaw tightened under his loose jowls. "I see nothing has changed. Frankly, I'm disappointed, Sadie. I thought you were smarter than to fall for his lies again. I won't be here to pick you up when he leaves you again."

And he turned on his heel and stormed off. Sadie glared after him. "You weren't there the first time—not that I wanted you, asshat."

She shrugged my arm off and whirled around to give me that same glare. "What the hell were you thinking of? Telling Devon Paxton that we were going to the reunion together. Everyone will know by morning."

Honestly, it had originally been nothing more than a way to piss off the asshole. I didn't like the way he was undressing Sadie and disrespecting her in front of me, so yeah, I had to do something. Then I couldn't have him know I didn't have a date for the reunion, the one I hadn't even remembered that was coming up.

I shrugged. "He insulted you."

She made a sound of disgust. "He always does that. I can handle him. It's you I have a problem with now."

I put on a wounded face. "I'm hurt. Did you already have a date to the reunion?"

"Would it matter?"

Before I could reply that hell, yes it would matter, old Mrs. Hubbard stepped in between us, unceremoniously pushing Sadie aside with her generous behind. She was a tall woman, generously proportioned in all ways and given to wearing floral muumuus as her signature attire. To go with her brand, she said, as a florist. All I knew was she hadn't changed in all the years I had known her. She still smelled like Shalimar and irises. I swear she owned stock in that company because I didn't think they made that perfume anymore. When she died, they would find boxes and boxes of the stuff in her basement.

She took my arm in a surprisingly firm grip. "Jaxon Bigsly. I was so pleased to hear that you'd finally come to your senses and come back home to us. It's been far too long. Your poor mother would have been heartbroken to think you'd left for so long."

Sadie smirked behind Mrs. Hubbard and folded her arms across her chest, waiting to see my reaction. Two could play the charm game. "I know, but I had to leave to make something of myself. I had to learn everything I could so I could come back here and do right by Tap Meister."

Her severe expression softened, and she patted my cheek while Sadie looked on in disbelief. "Oh, my dear boy. You've always been such a credit to this town. State champions. Home-coming king. Valedictorian. We had such hopes for you."

"I wasn't valedictorian, Mrs. Hubbard. That was Sadie. I was runner-up that time." I winked at her with a quick grin to show there were no hard feelings and gestured at Sadie behind her.

Mrs. Hubbard turned her head and blinked as if seeing Sadie for the first time. "Right, well. The point is, you shouldn't have stayed away. I don't know what happened between you two kids, but you were supposed to be married by now. I had your wedding bouquets and boutonnieres all picked out for you. Then you never came back."

"I never left, Mrs. Hubbard," Sadie piped up helpfully, and I shot her a glare.

The older woman gave me a considering look. "Maybe it was something you did, young man. Well, I hope you have it all figured out and are here to stay. Now you call me when you need flowers. For apologies or whatnot."

With a last look at Sadie, she glided off in a puff of Shalimar. I valiantly held in my sneeze until she was a safe distance away.

"Bless you," Sadie said.

"Thanks. Now about this date of yours."

"I don't have a date," she admitted, refusing to look at me. "Not yet."

"I hear Devon Paxton is available," I replied helpfully. "And I sense he's quite willing and eager to go with you."

She rolled her eyes and scanned the rapidly dwindling crowd. "Not in this lifetime. I planned on going solo."

I lifted an eyebrow. "When you have me right here? And you know Paxton will tell everyone that we're going together."

She sighed, a heavily put-upon sound. "Don't remind me."

"I'm clearly a better date than no one—or Paxton."

The more I thought about it, the more I realized how perfect this was. I had been looking for a way to get Sadie to spend time with me, and what better way than a pretend date with all of our high school friends? She would remember how good we were together, and if she forgot, there would be plenty of people there to remind her. And I could be sure to be my charming self. I had learned a few tricks in my time in Lovelorn from Drew Cafferty, but I had my own charm—and I had one other advantage. I knew Sadie.

She sighed again and looked at me, reluctance written in every line of her face. "I don't suppose I have a choice."

I dropped my arm around her shoulders and pulled her next to me. "Don't think so negatively. We might win reunion king and queen!"

"Oh God."

CHAPTER THIRTEEN

SADIE

I had escaped Jaxon for the better part of a week, but my luck had run out at the Council meeting. He wasn't wrong, though. I should have asked him if he was willing to sponsor the Biergarten, especially since I hadn't gotten another sponsor lined up. I may have identified a few options but had not spoken with anyone yet. I had hoped Jed would change his mind. He was notoriously cranky about doing things, then always came through. We did this song and dance every year, at least for the past three years that I'd run the festival, so I always assumed he would change his mind. Then when Jaxon bought the brewery, I should have called him, but I took the coward's way out. Avoidance, Sadie Taylor's strategy of choice for the better part of a decade.

I was rearranging the display case for the tenth time that week when the door flung open, bells jingling alarmingly. I looked up, and Lila stood there, her eyes wide.

"You're dating my brother? When did this happen?"

"Forget when. How did this happen?" Another voice spoke from behind her, pushing Lila into the shop, revealing my other friend and fellow business owner in town, Samantha Reed. Sam owned a hair salon, and I ducked all the changes she'd been wanting me to make to my look for years. It didn't stop us from being friends, though.

"Devon sure likes to talk, doesn't he?" I muttered, straightening from my position behind the display counter.

"I had to hear it over at Brewed Awakenings from Sabrina. For future reference, these are the things you call about. Not text, not email. Call. Immediately. I don't care how late it is." Lila waved her phone in the air to emphasize her words.

Sam stopped next to her, arms folded, and nodded once. "Ditto. In fact, we may need a group chat for this. I hope you updated Clara. She's going to be pissed she missed this news."

At that moment, the employee entrance door banged open. "Never mind. I sense she's aware."

Clara burst through the backroom door into the storefront and stopped dead when she saw us. She planted her hands on her hips. "You're dating Jaxon Bigsly?"

"Old news." Lila waved her hand. "The real question is, how did this happen?"

Okay, I needed to get control of the situation before it spun out of control, or more out of control than it already was. "We're not dating. It was stupid. We were at the council meeting. Devon was being an ass, like usual, and asked me to the reunion in front of Jaxon. Jaxon sort of implied we were going together, and I didn't deny it."

The last was sort of mumbled, and I hoped no one heard it. But of course my friends all had the hearing of a bat and seized on it like a lifeline. Lila was the first to react. "Oh my God. You're going to the reunion with him? This is epic!"

Sam gave me an evil smile. "Now you definitely need that makeover that you've been avoiding for years. You're going to make him beg for mercy before I'm done."

"Girls' night!"

*A*nd that's how I found myself in Samantha's salon after hours, my hair done up with some weird goop that I feared would turn into some strange color, and my alleged friends were sitting around finishing off their third bottle of wine, laughing and scrolling through online shopping sites, trying to find me a dress to make Jaxon's jaw drop.

We had a girls' night at least once a month and rotated locations between all of us. Samantha Reed, who owned the salon, usually hosted her turn at her salon, and we did facials and nails or other spa-type activities. Tonight, it seemed, everyone was focused on me. Lucky me.

It didn't matter that I had no intention of making Jaxon beg or whatever they wanted. In fact, I planned on backing out of the whole thing. First, I needed a good excuse, one that wouldn't make me look like I was scared to go out with him.

Lila nudged Sam from their side-by-side position. "She's panicking."

Sam nodded sagely and poured more wine, spilling a little. "Yup. Total panic."

"Shouldn't you be a little sober since you're coloring my hair hot pink or purple or whatever the hell this color is?"

Sam waved her hand. "I've only had two glasses. I'm fine. And your color won't be weird, although you would look banging with some pink highlights."

Clara and Lila turned excited eyes on me, but I shut that shit down immediately. "Absolutely not. I am a respectable business-woman. No pink highlights. Normal colors, please."

Sam sighed. "Fine. We're just brightening up your natural color then putting in some amazing highlights. You're going to be the talk of the reunion. And Jaxon will regret ever walking away."

"He already does," Lila put in. "Why do you think he's back?"

"So if you're not interested in Jaxon, why the makeover?" Courtney Maddux asked from her position lying across several chairs, her legs over the arm of the end, swinging hard.

"Exactly my point." I still wasn't sure how I'd ended up here either, though it felt nice to have a girls' night and be pampered.

"You could always nab Devon," Sam said with a sly smile.

The sip of wine and the cheese from the charcuterie board threatened to rise up. "Definitely not."

"Interesting that you never considered him when you were searching for a date. He's our age, available, and would love to date you," Courtney said.

So much for Courtney's "matchmaking" skills. She'd probably pair me with Devon in a photo shoot. "More to get back at Jaxon than out of any genuine interest in me," I countered. "He's always competed with Jaxon. I'm just one of the toys they fought over."

"Not to Jaxon," Lila said quietly.

"No, not to him," I agreed. "Okay, ladies. How do I handle this reunion situation? I can't go with Jaxon, but I can't back out, either."

Sam came over and tested my hair. "Time to wash. I don't know why you don't give it a shot. It's one night. You have a date, so you don't have to deal with the whispers or creepy Devon hitting on you, and it's over. No big deal."

Her hands massaging my scalp felt amazing. I closed my eyes and sank into the feeling, while praying she hadn't turned my hair pink. "I suppose you're right. How bad could it be?"

She escorted me to her chair, and the mirror was covered. "No seeing the end result until we're done."

Sam started cutting, and the girls showed me dress after dress as options for the reunion. They finally threatened to pick one and show up with it. We settled on a red wrap-style dress that I thought was too revealing but Lila declared would be perfect. I ordered it before I could second-guess myself. I'd blame the wine for any misjudgment.

Finally, Sam finished, and Lila pulled the towel off the mirror with a flourish. My jaw dropped. No pink in sight. Just honey blond and streaks of lighter blond. My hair, instead of straight, now swung just to my shoulders in soft waves, with chunky streaks of blond. I could still put it up when I was working and for Chelsea's wedding, but it looked amazing when it was down now, not the blah, boring Sadie Taylor.

"I love it," I breathed. Everyone let out a breath and clapped high-fives.

Now to survive the reunion.

CHAPTER FOURTEEN

JAXON

I spread out in the reception area. Word hadn't gotten out that we were open for business yet. Besides, it was during the week, so we had fewer customers to drop in for beer tastings. I had an office, one I hadn't really settled into yet. I'd never really enjoyed being in an office, shut away from the action going on in the brewery. I had spent most of my career on the floor, checking the batches, the brews, bottling, anything going on, though every part of the process usually had their own manager. Now I oversaw everything plus the brewery management, though Sean would focus on the business side—distribution, sales, any type of expansion we might decide to do.

Brewing was taking a backseat to everything else that had to be done to get Tap Meister up to speed. Sean and I had worked out a priority list while he was in town, which were really thinly veiled *ignore these at your own risk* recommendations. Sean could be a bossy sonofabitch at times. But he knew what he was doing, so I was sitting here, trying to figure out how to do some of these.

The door opened, and two children's voices echoed in the

space. Ella stumbled as she tried to keep up with her brother and be the first to reach me. "Uncle Jax! We came for a visit!"

"But not to drink beer because it's yucky." Caleb made a face, but he waited for his sister to catch up before they both clambered onto chairs on either side of me at the table.

"Whatcha doing?" Ella leaned across the table, half on and half off, her feet on the chair.

This was why I'd moved back home. I had missed so much while I was building my knowledge and experience. I didn't regret it, but I missed seeing them grow up. Hopefully Lila was on board with adding a third rugrat to the family as she'd been talking about so I could prove to be a better uncle in the future.

Being the efficient mother she was, Lila whipped out a spread worthy of preschool kids. Crackers, cheese, fruit. All finger foods, along with juice boxes and plenty of napkins and wipes for sticky hands and faces. I was more than happy to put aside the paperwork for the impromptu picnic. I wasn't avoiding anything, not at all.

Once the picnic was over, Lila had shifted us to another table, leaving her kids playing quietly. Well, sort of. Caleb was doing something with plastic dinosaurs, and Ella had a doll that she was talking to.

"God, that sends me back. Though I don't think we were that well behaved."

Lila laughed. "I seem to recall you ripping Chloe's head off and replacing it with your stuffed bear's head one night. I woke up with something from the Godfather."

I laughed, remembering her screams and wails the next morning. "If you remember, you started it by ripping Teddy's head off first. I was just getting even."

"Dad didn't think so."

I winced. "I can still feel that belt on my ass."

She whacked me on my shoulder. "Baby. It wasn't that bad."

I gave her a wounded look. "What would you know, Dad's

delicate princess? All you had to do was stick out your lower lip and feign tears and you got whatever you wanted."

She glared at me, then we both laughed. "You're right. Dad tiptoed around me, especially after Mom died."

"Yeah, he didn't want to talk about girl stuff. Can you imagine?"

Lila shuddered. "Imagine it? I had to live it. One day, he threw several boxes of tampons and pads in my room and ran. I didn't even know what they were for. I had cut my knee, and there was blood in the bathroom. I guess he thought I got my period."

I snort-laughed. "I can beat that. Picture Dad talking about sex and condoms."

She groaned. "At least he never tried to do that with me. He said, don't do it and avoided all talk after that."

"Classic Dad. Avoided anything he didn't like," I sighed.

Impulsively, Lila reached across the table and hugged me. "I'm so glad you're home. Now what's got you down? Can I help?"

Damn, I had to get back to work. Time was ticking on these tasks, and I had to get them going. Actually, I eyed Lila, who met my gaze innocently. She was perfect.

"If you mean it, I could use some of your party planning expertise. I have a grand opening to plan."

Lila's laughter echoed in the space, and even her kids paused and looked over at us. "It's not that funny. You had the best parties for the kids. I may not have been to all of them, but I saw pictures. Caleb's last party was pirates, and Ella's was mermaid themed. Seriously, I need your organization and creativity for this."

By now, she was laughing so hard that she could barely breathe. She bent over, wheezing and snort-laughing, and I was honestly worried that I'd have to dig into the emergency kit and pray the oxygen tank worked. I was also getting more than a little pissed off, so I sat there and let her partially asphyxiate herself until she regained control.

Finally, she wiped the tears from her eyes with a napkin. "Oh, I needed that laugh. I forgot you hadn't come home for the last couple of parties. I didn't plan those. If I had, we'd be lucky to have cake. No, Sadie organized everything, from the theme to the decorations to the invitations and the food. She was the rock star of the whole thing. Why do you think she runs half the festivals in town?"

Of course. Why didn't I realize that? I knew Lila could forget where she put her phone while she was talking on it. More times that I could count, I could hear her looking for something, and when I'd ask, she'd tell me her cell, and I'd ask her what she was using. Lila was wicked smart, but wasn't the best at organizing anything.

Sadie, on the other hand, had been our class president, planned our prom and probably the reunion, too. She had volunteered for the charity drives at school and was ruthless when it came to preparing for anything. She'd be ideal to help with this because she also knew the people in town who could help me. But there was one problem.

"She'll never help me."

Lila popped a grape in her mouth. "You'll never know until you ask. And this is the perfect way to get close to her and show her how you've changed."

Valid point.

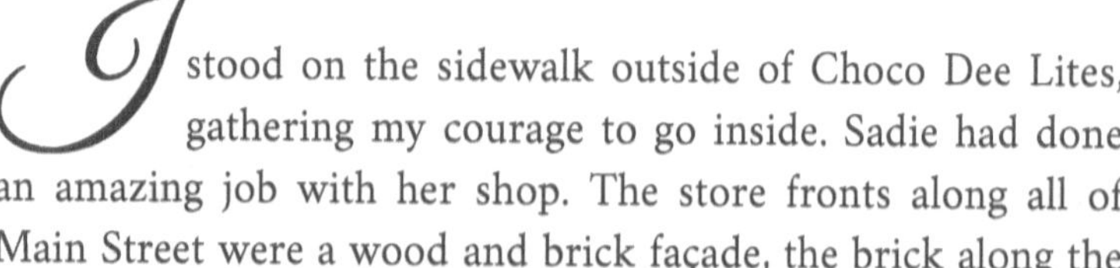

I stood on the sidewalk outside of Choco Dee Lites, gathering my courage to go inside. Sadie had done an amazing job with her shop. The store fronts along all of Main Street were a wood and brick façade, the brick along the second story and above, while around the store fronts themselves there were colorful wood facings to enhance the historic feel of the village.

Sadie's store front was particularly bright and colorful to draw in customers to her shop. The wood was painted a bright lavender, and her store name was in gold lettering. The door looked like a typical house door, painted lavender, with a sectioned window at the top and solid at the bottom. There were several open windows to see inside and a display case on the inside showing off fancy chocolates that made my mouth water. A swag of flowers and greens stretched across the store front between the sign and the window to add a touch of whimsey. It was so Sadie. Fun, bright, happy.

She loved Holly Creek. I always knew that. She wouldn't have been happy living anywhere else, even for a short time. And I hadn't known if I would ever come back, though, if I wanted to be honest with myself, I was always coming back. I needed Sadie, and I wanted Tap Meister. They were both in my blood, deeply ingrained in me, a part of me. I had one. Now to convince the other to give me a chance.

"Welcome back, Jaxon! I'm so happy you're here." I turned and gave an automatic smile at the three people, all my father's age, who stood there, gazing at me expectantly. I wished I recognized them, but after ten years away, well, my memory was a little fuzzy.

One woman ignored my confusion and hugged me. Her pillowy frame swallowed me, and I refrained from coughing from the heavy floral perfume, though it did trigger a memory. "Mrs. Casciello. Are you still working at the high school library?"

"No, I retired a few years ago. Your class ran me ragged. But we sure missed you. Will you be helping with the football team this fall?"

Football. I hadn't thought about football since I blew out my shoulder in pre-season training at Syracuse. It was never the same, but I always knew I wasn't meant to play professional football, despite my father's dreams. My plans lay in different directions, and the shoulder injury helped me get there sooner. Hell, if I hadn't gotten hurt, I wouldn't have met Sean and found an actual path forward. But Holly Creek still saw me as the quarterback who led them to the championship, nothing more.

"Sorry, Mrs. Casciello. I'll be pretty busy getting Tap Meister up and running."

She scowled at me, as did her two companions, older like her, though they were dressed more conservatively. One woman was tall, painfully thin, wearing red pants and a floral top and matching bright red lipstick. The other was short, like Mrs. Casciello, and somewhat plump, wearing a white sleeveless top and pink shorts. They looked vaguely familiar, but again, I had been away a long time, sneaking into town for my sister and dad occasionally and back out. I wouldn't recognize my own classmates, most likely.

"Come on, May. Let the poor boy see Sadie. They have a lot to catch up on. Remember to grovel. My Harry usually does flowers and dinner when he has to apologize." The thin woman pointedly stared at my empty hands. Well, empty except for the notebook.

"I'm working on it, ladies. Now, if you'll excuse me." I gestured to the door of Sadie's shop, and they giggled and hustled on past.

I sucked in a deep breath and let it out slowly. Then I pushed open the door, and a bell jingled cheerily in the space. The interior was as open and welcoming as the exterior. Bright white and accent colors of purple and green, it had floral arrangements to lend a delicate touch. The chocolate was displayed in glass counters and made my mouth water just looking at the options. Sadie was bent over behind the counter arranging a tray of truffles and straightened with a bright smile that faded when she saw me.

"Oh, it's you."

"I guess I asked for that, dropping by unannounced after ten years." I tried to lighten the mood, but judging by the flat way she looked at me, it didn't work. "Look, Lila suggested I reach out and ask for your help."

She arched an eyebrow. "My help?"

Damn it. "What do I need to do to get you to forgive me?"

She blinked, clearly startled by my statement, then looked chagrined. She came around the display counter to stand in front of me. "I'm sorry, Jaxon. I'm trying. I think I'm still in shock that you're back."

A strand of her hair had fallen out of her ponytail and, without thinking, I reached out and tucked it behind her ear. The honey blond strand looked lighter than the last time I'd seen her. "Did you do something different with your hair? I like it."

She blushed. "Yeah, Sam Reed at Dye Cut Works gave me highlights for the reunion and a haircut. Apparently, it was part of some makeover scheme or something."

"I like it. You know I'm staying, right? I'm not leaving this time." My heart twisted at the vulnerability in her eyes.

We stood there for a long minute. Finally, her eyes dropped. "I know. I'm trying."

"Then help me."

She nodded. "What do you need?"

Relief flooded me, but I tried not to show it. "I want to have a grand reopening for Tap Meister. It's probably stupid, but we want to invite people to taste some of our new brews, see that we're staying and planning on growing in Holly Creek. Except..."

A smile crossed her face. "Except you suck at party planning."

I shrugged, a sheepish smile on my face. "It's kind of a family trait. But I hear you're a genius at it. So can you help me?"

She shook her head but was smiling the whole time. That's when I knew I had her. "When is it? How many people? What have you done so far?"

I pulled out my notebook. "Labor Day weekend, a couple of weeks from now. I know it's a quick turnaround, but we're doing it for the town, really."

"How will you have any beer ready by then? Doesn't it take weeks to brew beer?" She wrinkled her nose, and I remembered she had never been a big fan of the taste of beer but would listen patiently when I would talk about the brewing process.

"We'd been in discussion with Jed for months. He let me brew some of my recipes to prepare for finalizing the deal."

She arched a brow. "That's pretty risky, isn't it? He could have backed out and kept your product."

I nodded. "But we had an agreement that if the deal fell through, I would get a portion of the profits from the new brews."

She scowled suddenly, as if an idea had suddenly occurred to her. "If he had the deal in the works and new brews, why did he bail on the Biergarten?"

"How would I know why Jed does anything? He should have told me and given me the chance to decide, but he didn't. Maybe he's just a cranky old man who likes to screw with people."

She laughed, the sound familiar and refreshing. "You're right. That sounds like something Jed would do. Okay, I'm in. I'll help you. Because it helps the town."

I didn't care why she was in. She'd agreed to spend time with me, and I could work with that. "Excellent. How about we start tonight over dinner?"

CHAPTER FIFTEEN

SADIE

I wasn't exactly sure how this happened, but I had a date with Jaxon. I could tell myself it was a working dinner, helping him with his open house, but if that was the case, we'd have done it at the shop or his brewery. That we were going to dinner at all meant this was something more, and I wasn't sure what I thought about it.

Who was I kidding? My brain told me this was a crazy idea. My heart screamed to be careful, but my body was all in. I'd had more dreams about Jaxon since Lovelorn than I'd had since we'd broken up, reminders of the man he'd grown into, the very sexy man who still watched me like he wanted to devour me. And my body was all on board with that. My heart was even softening as he said things that I wanted to hear. Things like *he wanted to win me back. He was staying in town. He came back for me.* What woman wouldn't melt at those words?

I was no exception, and here I was, sitting at a window table in the fanciest restaurant in Holly Creek, at the same place where I'd had so many failed dates, across from the one man I'd never really gotten over. Was I really considering taking a second chance? Because that was what tonight was really about, a second chance. We may have said this was about his grand reopening, but, judging by the heated look in Jaxon's eyes, the brewery was the last thing on his mind. Unless he thought beer was sexy. Which he probably did, now that I thought about it.

I took a sip of my wine to steady my nerves. Jaxon looked so different from when we used to date. He had grown a bit of a beard, close to his skin, but enough to make me wonder how it would feel on my skin when we made love. He hadn't had much of a scruff back when we were dating, so the facial hair was a major turn-on, something I hadn't expected. His body had filled out considerably, though he had always been strong and muscular thanks to his years of playing football. But working around the beer barrels and kegs, along with age, had helped him grow into an incredibly sexy man a few inches over six feet, just enough to let me wear heels and still feel feminine next to him.

I had never been a petite girl, liking my own baking and cooking too much for that. And now that I made chocolate, well, the old adage was true. Never trust a skinny cook. But I was trying to be careful with the wedding coming up in a few months. Speaking of which, maybe I had the date solution in front of me.

Jaxon sprawled in his chair, the gentle light making him look even sexier, if that was possible. Damn him. My heart skipped a beat. I hadn't expected to be sitting here with him ever again. And now I couldn't help but think about Clara's words to consider giving him a chance.

"So about this grand reopening. What were you thinking?"

He sighed and set his beer down. "We're starting with business? Okay. Honestly, I don't know. We're already open and not changing much, so I don't know that we want to do a lot. But I want to show everyone that Tap Meister is growing and expanding and here to stay, if that makes sense."

I nodded, considering his words. "Jed was a fixture in town, having run the brewery for decades. But we all knew it was slowly running down. Frankly, I was surprised at some of the upgrades in recent months. We had my friend Chelsea's bridal gathering there in July, and the reception room was nice."

Jaxon nodded, absently swirling his beer. "We made some suggestions before taking over. I even asked about brewing some new recipes as we were working out the deal to set us up for success. Unconventional, but we didn't want to lose the whole summer season. Jed was a little difficult in the negotiation process."

I took a sip of my wine. "Well, he was probably holding out hope that his son would take over. But we all knew his son would sell as soon as he could."

Jaxon grinned. "We made a generous offer. He'd have been a fool to reject us. And at least Jed got the money and not his son. But honestly, Oktoberfest is probably our real opening, and this one will be a soft launch, just for the town and any tourists in the area."

I loved that idea and softened my heart a bit further, showing how Jaxon was considering the town in his plans. Damn it. "I love it. You could cater a very simple event. Appetizers and a beer tasting of your newest brews, if they'll be ready. Invite the town. Offer a stamp card for people to try the beers you have, a stamp per type of beer, maybe. Then you can renew it next season."

His eyes brightened. "Oh, like a passport program. I love that."

I nodded. "You could also have voting on the next beer flavor or recipe or whatever you call it. Winner gets naming rights or something. And of course swag, giveaways with your logo and name. Helps spread the word."

He leaned forward, clearly getting excited about the ideas flowing. "Do you really think we can get all of this done in time?"

I let out a breath. "It won't be easy but, since you're keeping it local, sure. What's your social media presence for the brewery?"

He looked chagrined. "Beats the hell out of me."

I laughed. "Figure it out. Hell, hire a high school kid. They offer internships through the school for kids to learn about business. Trust me, it's worth it. Those kids can help you boost your presence in no time. Maybe not quickly enough for the opening, but by Oktoberfest, you'll be in good shape. I'll send you the contact information for the program coordinator tomorrow."

He reached across the table and took my hand, cradling it in his. "Thank you so much, Sadie. Seriously, I don't know what I would do without you."

My hand tingled in his, warmth spreading from where he was cradling it. My face heated, and I looked down, avoiding his gaze. "Glad to help. I'm always willing to help another business be successful in Holly Creek. It helps us all succeed."

He tugged gently, and I met his gaze. "That's not it, and you know it. I know this isn't easy for you. Thank you."

The waitress chose that moment to deliver our meals, and we broke to eat. We made idle chit-chat throughout the meal, catching up on our friends and what had been going on since we'd last seen each other years before. It seemed so impersonal, like a true business dinner, if not for the occasional heated look Jaxon sent me. It felt so familiar, like no time had passed at all, and I found myself relaxing and enjoying the dinner, like I hadn't enjoyed a date in a long time.

Not that this was a date. No, this was a business dinner, I reminded myself. We just happened to have dinner at the same time because he was lonely and didn't want to eat alone, right? Sure, that was it. He couldn't eat with his sister and her adorable yet messy children every night, and I knew how his father was, with his bitterness about life.

"Have you seen your dad?"

Jaxon grimaced. "The one topic guaranteed to bring the evening down. Yes, I've seen my father. He's made his feelings well known about my life's choices."

I took a sip of my wine. "But you bought Tap Meister. I would think he would be thrilled since he worked there."

Jaxon took a deep breath and swirled his beer in his glass, staring out the large picture window into the parking lot. After a few minutes of silence, broken only by the murmur of patrons eating, the clinking of silverware on plates and glassware, he finally spoke. "I don't know how often you've spoken to my father since I left, but I'm not his favorite person, not since I decided not to play college football."

I frowned, remembering our tearful goodbye when he left early for training camp at Syracuse University. I thought I wouldn't see him for months because of the rigors of training camp and the season, but then he'd gotten hurt a few weeks later. His surgery and rehabilitation had taken all season, and I had driven to the university frequently that year to visit. He had been depressed and moody, but I thought it was about his injury. When he broke up with me, I had thought he needed time to come to terms with not playing football anymore. But he had decided not to play on his own?

"I don't understand. You chose not to play football anymore?"

CHAPTER SIXTEEN

JAXON

 had hoped tonight could be a turning point for us, a date night with maybe a chance for a goodnight kiss. I certainly hadn't expected to share deep revelations or personal secrets that I had never planned to tell anyone. But Sadie had been there for me through my injury, and I had been a dick to her, as only a nineteen-year-old self-involved asshole could be. I was so wrapped up in hearing my father in one ear yelling about getting back on the field as soon as I could to take back the backup quarterback slot before sophomore year and my own gut telling me this wasn't what I wanted. I'd spent half the year drinking, and the rest depressed.

Thank goodness I'd met Sean. He pulled my ass out of the fire, somewhat literally, and gave me a direction and the confidence to pursue it.

Before I could respond, though, the past reared its ugly head in the form of my old football coach, Mike Thompson. He had aged in the decade since I'd last seen him, put on weight, and had much less hair than he'd had back when he was my coach, though he'd had a buzz cut, so it was pretty non-existent then too.

His shadow loomed above me, with his wife next to him. He clapped me on the shoulder, and I winced at the heavy hand. "Jaxon Bigsly! I'd heard you'd moved back, but I hadn't seen you. How have you been?"

I ignored the subtle rebuke in his tone. Coach Thompson had been a guiding mentor in my life, but I hadn't seen him in years, not since I'd disappointed him by not playing football at Syracuse. Yeah, I had a good reason, but I'd never explained it to him. I stood, manners having been ingrained in me, first by my mom, then by this man right here. We shook hands. "Good to see you, Coach. Mrs. Thompson. I've only been back a couple of weeks. Been busy getting settled with the brewery."

He nodded. "I'd heard you bought Tap Meister from Jed. That's a good move. You'll do good things there and really help the town. You'll bring your star quality to it and your leadership, just like you did on the team back in high school."

I winced at the subtle reminder of our championship. "I'll do my best, sir."

"Call me Mike, son. You're no longer my student. How's the shoulder? Too bad about Syracuse. You could have gone all the way."

That was the trouble with small towns. They forgot nothing and had their own kind of memory, even if it was faulty. I had been a decent football player, a damned good one. But going pro? That was highly unlikely even if I hadn't blown out my shoulder. I knew that. Even during training camp at Syracuse, I was always going to be a backup quarterback. The starter ended up going pro, and he was light-years ahead of me in skill and talent.

He also wanted it more.

But Coach wouldn't see it that way, so I humored him, let him believe he'd coached a possible pro-baller. I rotated my shoulder for effect. "Well, it still lets me know when weather is coming."

We both laughed at the old athletes' corny joke. "Well, I'll let you and Sadie get back to your dinner. I was sure sorry to hear you broke up back then. Maybe this is a reunion of sorts?" He winked at us.

"Oh, you old fool. Leave them alone. Ignore him. Have a nice night, Jaxon and Sadie." Mrs. Thompson ushered the coach out of the restaurant before I had to respond.

I sat back down and faced Sadie. She had a small smile playing around her lips. "How many people have asked you about football and coming home?"

"More than I care to count," I admitted, taking a deep swallow of my beer.

"You never told him about your injury, that you could have played?"

I set my beer down. It was time for some truths. Sadie deserved them. "No, I never told him. The docs said I could play but, if I played and got hurt again, I would seriously fuck up my shoulder, possibly beyond repair. But I could play again if I wanted."

I waited to see if she would pick up the thread. But of course, Sadie, who often knew me better than I knew myself, saw right through it.

"But you didn't."

I shook my head. "I liked football, enjoyed playing it. But I couldn't see myself playing it forever. Unfortunately, my father wanted to see his son on Saturday television, playing college ball, then on Sunday afternoon in the pros."

This time, Sadie reached out for me, taking my hand in hers and gripping it tightly. "That was his dream for you."

I gave a raw, harsh laugh. "I wish it were that simple. No, that was his dream for him. I was following in his footsteps, a mini-Darren. I'm surprised he didn't name me after himself, except he hated his name."

Sadie grew quiet, and the waitress came and cleared the

table, leaving the dessert menu. We both ordered coffees, and I saw her linger over the chocolate flourless cake. I gestured to the waitress and ordered it with two forks. Sadie ducked her head but smiled.

Once we were alone, she looked at me. "Is that why you left?"

Like I said, she was perceptive. "I couldn't take the pressure. Dad wanted me to be a professional football player. The town kept talking about when they could erect a sign saying they knew me when or *Jaxon Bigsly was born here*. I was going to put Holly Creek on the map. It fucking sucked."

God, I hated whining. Poor me. I had all this success and people liked me. But it got to where I didn't know who I was anymore. The waitress brought the coffee and the cake. I doctored my coffee with a little cream, no sugar. Sadie automatically poured cream and sugar in hers, absently stirring the liquid and staring at the cake. But I didn't think she really saw it.

I picked up the fork and cut a piece of the decadent dessert and held it to her lips. "I'm sure this isn't as good as the chocolate at this amazing store in town, but it will suffice since the shop is closed."

A smile teased the corner of her lips, and she opened her mouth, letting me slide the bite into it. She closed over it and moaned, her eyes closing. Her expression sent a bolt of lust through me. My pants tightened, and I was glad I was sitting at the table so no one could see.

She slowly opened her mouth. "That was so good. I need to get the recipe."

I grinned. "I thought chefs never shared their secrets."

She scowled. "Hayes Kelley owns this place, and he owes me a favor. I think it's time to collect."

I grinned, glad she had moved off of the topic of my father and failed dreams. We demolished the cake and our coffee. While I was paying the bill, Sadie hunted Hayes down. I saw her corner him over by the hostess stand. I didn't envy him at that moment, especially since I knew she was leaving with me. Well, she was walking out with me. We had met there, and I would have to let her drive home. Alone.

I had not thought this through.

Sadie returned, looking thoroughly disgruntled. I stifled a grin. "He won't share, huh?"

"Shut up," she muttered, stalking past me outside.

I was going to get her that recipe. Somehow.

I followed Sadie to her car, and we stood there awkwardly. I really wanted to kiss her, but I sensed this could go either way. So I buried my hands in my pockets to keep myself from reaching for her.

"Thanks for your suggestions. I'll get started on them right away." She nodded, still studying me in a weird way, like she was trying to figure something out. "What?"

She shook her head. "No, I'm just replaying the last ten years or so in my head."

I winced. "Yeah, that is not how I wanted tonight to go. I want to move past that, not relive it."

She laid a hand on my arm, the second time she'd voluntarily reached out to me. "But our past is a part of us, a part of how we got here. We have to deal with it before we move on. No, I'm thinking of all the times I put pressure on you to stay, to do certain things. I never imagined what you were going through."

I pulled her close, willing her to understand what I was about to say. "Sadie, you never put any pressure on me that I minded. I wasn't ready to settle down and get married. But I'm sure if I asked you to wait, you would have. It was never about you. It was always me. You have to understand that."

She cocked her head, a soft smile on her face. "For the first time, I think I believe that. But I don't think it was all about you, either. You were put in an untenable position and didn't see a way out. You wanted to make your own choices, whatever they were. I respect that, Jaxon. You've done well for yourself. You should be proud."

My jaw slackened as I stared at her, at the words I never expected to hear. "Does this mean you forgive me?"

She thought for a moment. "Yes, I think I do. I forgive you. I'm happy with how my life has turned out. I love my shop, where I live, my friends. And you're right. I wasn't ready before now to settle down to marriage and a family. Maybe it was for the best that we took some time to grow up."

My heart pounded in my chest as I took in the possibilities. I willed myself to calm the fuck down. At least my voice remained steady. "Do you think we could give ourselves a second chance?"

She raised up on tiptoes and brushed her lips across mine. "I'd like that."

I stood there stunned for a moment as she smirked at me. "Oh hell no, Sadie. That's not a kiss."

I crowded her against the car and did what I had been dying to do since the moment I saw her in Lovelorn. The night was pitch black, and the parking lot was quiet, with only the distant sound of cicadas and peepers in the night. The sound of conversation and music was muffled from inside the restaurant, but it felt like we were alone out here, private, and I took my chance.

I stepped closer, my heart racing with anticipation. I had been waiting for this moment for the past ten years. I closed the distance between us until she was pressed against me. My hands gently cupped her face, her skin soft and inviting beneath my fingertips, and her beauty took my breath away. Our lips were mere millimeters apart, and the energy between us was palpable. I closed my eyes, feeling everything around us disappear. I opened my eyes again, my gaze locked with Sadie's. I wanted to make sure she was ready for this.

Slowly, I leaned in. My lips met hers, and I kissed her with a passion that had been missing for the past ten years. The feeling of being reunited with the one my heart belonged to was nothing short of magical. Our tongues met, intertwining in a waltz that felt like a homecoming.

We kissed until the world around us became blurry, and all I could focus on was the warmth of her lips against mine. I knew I could stay in this moment forever, an eternity in her embrace with my lips sealed against hers. Sadie's hands moved up the back of my neck, her fingertips barely grazing my skin as if she was afraid to let go. I pulled away, both of us reluctantly breaking the precious bond between us.

We stood there, taking each other in, unwilling to break the silence. I brushed my fingertips against her cheek, our eyes locking for one last embrace. Laughter erupted into the silence as the door to the restaurant opened and a group of people burst into the parking lot. We sprang apart, looking all kinds of guilty, but no one even spared us a glance.

I cleared my throat. "Are you okay to drive?"

She nodded and opened her car door with a beep. "Thanks for dinner. I'll send you the information I promised tomorrow."

I nodded and stepped back as she slipped into her car and then slowly drove out of the parking lot. I buried my hands in my pockets and headed for my car, whistling. I had a chance to win her back. Now to head for home and a cold shower.

CHAPTER SEVENTEEN

SADIE

I played that kiss on rewind for the next several days. It haunted my nights and preoccupied my days as I reevaluated my situation with Jaxon. I spoke with him periodically, answering questions and giving him ideas for his grand reopening, but he kept his distance. I hadn't expected that, and it threw me off balance. I'd thought he would show up at my shop, or my house, asking me out, flirting, but he was perfectly businesslike and responsible.

It was pissing me off.

"What flew up your skirt and lodged in your ass?" Clara asked from the other end of the counter.

I straightened after rearranging the truffles. "Nice imagery. I just need to fix the truffles. They weren't quite balanced."

She gave me a look of pure disbelief. "You fixed them four times in the last half hour. What's going on?"

Like I was going to admit that I was annoyed that man I had resented moving back to town wasn't coming to see me, asking me out or anything. He had said he'd moved back to win me back, laid a kiss on me that scorched my nerve endings and woke up my hormones, then he walked away. But if I complained, Clara would know about the kiss, and then Lila would know, and I would never hear the end of it.

"I'm just nervous about Oktoberfest and the reunion tonight."

Clara grunted. "You have six weeks until Oktoberfest, so no worries there. But the reunion? I get that. My fifteen year is coming up, and I'm avoiding that one hard. I didn't like those people back then. Why would I hang out with them now, being all fake like I am happy to see them? Hard pass."

Clara came from a larger town in southern New York that she hadn't been able to wait to leave, and then had wandered for a few years before settling in Holly Creek. She didn't quite understand the small town, but she loved it here, despite its sometimes incestuous nature. I, on the other hand, loved the town and had enjoyed high school. I'd had several friends and couldn't wait to see some of them, though it would be very interesting with Jaxon at my side.

Most of them knew we had broken up a couple years after high school, so to see us together again, even just for one night, was going to start tongues wagging. I already had several customers in the shop asking me the status of our relationship, and even my mom asked if we were getting back together. We were always going to be Jaxon and Sadie, the golden couple. No one could ever see us as separate.

Of course, I was the fool who was working the day of the reunion instead of leaving it to my assistant, a fact she had lamented upon most of the day already. But I was ignoring her. I had my dress and plenty of time before the evening.

Before I could answer Clara, the door jingled, and we both looked over to see Bobby Macklemore, Mrs. Hubbard's grandson and part-time delivery guy, balancing an enormous bouquet that almost obscured his face. It certainly blinded his vision since he almost tripped and ran into the display case.

Clara shot me an amused glance. "I think those are for you. I never seem to date a guy who says anything with flowers."

"Yup, they sure are. I have the card here somewhere, Miss Taylor." The bouquet wobbled precariously, and I raced around the display case to grab it before it fell to the ground. "Thanks, Miss Taylor. Here you go."

He handed me the card and a plastic corsage box with a flourish and a big grin. I recognized the writing immediately, and my heart seized. "Would you like a couple of pieces of chocolate, Bobby?"

"Oh no, Miss Taylor. I couldn't do that." But he stared at the case longingly. I nudged him toward Clara, who pulled out a tray and let him pick a couple of pieces.

I took the bouquet full of beautiful and bright assorted flowers into the back room, where I could read the card in private.

Sadie,

Thanks for all of your help with the grand reopening. Here's a token of my gratitude. They made me think of you, bright, happy, and full of life.

I look forward to the reunion tonight. This is something to remember me by.

Jax

P.S. I'm still thinking about that kiss. I hope you are too.

My face burned as the swinging door opened behind me and Clara came in, chuckling quietly. "From Jaxon, I presume?"

I nodded, face hot. No way was I telling her about the kiss. But there was something I needed to do. "You have this, right? I have a reunion to prepare for."

Clara only grinned. "Sam already has an appointment for

you in thirty minutes. We were hoping you would come to that conclusion on your own."

I stared at her, fingering the end of my ponytail. "I already had my hair done and highlighted."

Clara gave me a dubious look. "There are other things that need managing. And you can't do your hair for shit, except in a ponytail. She'll do a much better job." She leaned forward and peered over my shoulder. "I hope that corsage matches your dress. Yup, it does."

I glared at her, suspicion blooming. "Did you tell Jaxon what I was wearing tonight?"

She gave me the appearance of all innocence. "How could I? You never showed me." She took the bouquet and bustled me toward the back door. "Now move. You're going to be late."

A few hours later, I had been pampered and fussed over until I barely recognized myself. My hair lay in soft waves around my face, brushing the tops of my shoulders. My makeup had been done by one of the girls at the salon, and it looked soft and beautiful. I really needed to get tips from her. And I wore a dress that I swore had not been in my closet that morning, while the one I had intended to wear had mysteriously disappeared. I wonder where it had gone.

But it was all worth it to see the stunned look on Jaxon's face when I opened the door. His jaw dropped, and his eyes heated in an instant. "Holy shit, Sadie. You look amazing. I'm afraid to kiss you now and mess it all up."

I felt the blush stain my cheek, and I toyed with the corsage at my wrist, a galaxy orchid decorated with sprigs of pearls. The purple and blue of the orchid accented my deep purple dress but would have suited the blue one I had expected to wear that night as well. But the purple silk wrap dress felt heavenly on my body, like it was tailored to me, showing off more of my figure than I was normally comfortable with and more skin than I liked. But, judging by Jaxon's heated gaze, he liked what he saw.

"Thank you for the corsage. You know we don't do that for reunions."

He took my hand. "I do. Are you ready?"

Electricity shot up my arm where he held my hand and he escorted me to his SUV, where he helped me into the passenger seat. Far from the days where I scrambled into his fifteen-year-old Toyota Celica and prayed the door would stay shut. He drove to the brewery where we were hosting the reunion, something I had been surprised about, but he had offered it as part of the soft launch re-opening.

The large open space had been cleaned and spruced up, the varnish on the wood beams redone so they almost shone in the warm light that he'd installed, instead of the harsh, cool white light that Jed had. The high-top tables were spread out, also in the darker wood, in sets of two- and four-seaters for people to gather around. Along the edge of the room were larger tables for bigger groups of eight to ten. Each table had varying sizes of electric candles on them or a hurricane lamp, in the case of the larger table, all throwing that warm light, but not with an actual flame. The ambiance was warm, inviting, casual. I loved it.

Impulsively, I turned and hugged Jaxon. "You've done a wonderful job here."

He grinned. "Thanks. Your advice really helped, along with some pictures and suggestions. And that high school student intern started this week and groaned when she saw our social media. I think she asked for a second helper. But we're on the map. On Facebook, Instagram, TikTok, and some other sites that I don't even know about."

I laughed. "You're sounding old, Jaxon. Even I know what those sites are."

He grimaced. "I don't have time to deal with that all of that. I don't know how you do it. We have enough to manage here with the beer, the distribution, the tastings, and the events."

"Well, my business is considerably smaller in scope than yours. You're thinking of adding events like these? Jed offered his space, but the people who rented it had to get all their own catering, decorations, and everything. We had my friend Chelsea's bridal get-together here, and it would have been so much easier to have someone onsite to help coordinate."

"Sean definitely sees us expanding. And I do, too. He's talking adding a restaurant and bar to go along with the tastings, though the timing on that is unknown, and definitely offering more events. He'd like to push for events that come with larger budgets. Make ourselves attractive to out-of-town brides looking for rustic elegance, city businesses interested in small-town charm, that sort of thing. The kitchen is sitting unused, though it seems to be in decent shape, the caterer for tonight used it, but Sean will get it checked for needed upgrades and to make sure it passes codes. He's already got a list."

I walked around the space, noting the wait staff making adjustments to some of the settings and the reunion committee also adding their own touches. Talk of expanding, restaurants and events all sounded like a long-term business plan, not a short-term whim. Both Jaxon and his business partner, Sean, definitely seemed like they were going to be hands-on owners, not absentee owners, content to let a manager run the place for them. I had met Sean Wallace briefly when he was in town previously, though I hadn't known exactly why he was in town. He seemed like a decent enough guy, but I wasn't sure if he would be content in a small town. Jaxon's words made me think they both were settling in.

I walked out onto the back patio, where the stone looked like it had been touched up with new settings. Jaxon followed me, a few steps behind. They had set up tables and chairs in case anyone wanted to sit outside in the beautiful summer evening, since it was still comfortable in late August. The trees along the patio had been decorated with strings of white light. In the distance, along the side of the building, the old water wheel that used to power the mill that this building once was also reflected the same decoration with lights along it.

"Are you keeping the wheel?"

"Yes. I consulted with a restoration specialist to see if it can be restored and even functional again. We don't need it for power, but it would be nice to see it turning again."

"You've done so much work in such a short time. I can't believe it."

"I've always known what I wanted," he said quietly from a few steps behind me.

His words arrowed into my heart, pricking at the old wound and bleeding a little. I turned. "Have you really? Then why did you leave?"

CHAPTER EIGHTEEN

JAXON

Before I could address the question, which deserved more than a flip answer, voices spilled out onto the patio, a bevy of people calling out to both of us, drawing us into the chaos that was our high school reunion. Sadie and I were pulled in different directions, torn in two like our lives had been for the past ten years. I didn't see much of her for the next hour or so.

"So what happened to you, man? One day you were headed pro and the next you disappeared."

"Is it true that when your shoulder blew out, you got addicted to pills and got kicked out of Syracuse?"

"I heard you got drafted but declined."

"I heard you were afraid to get hit again." That last statement was Devon Paxton, douchebag extraordinaire.

The constant barrage of questions about my shoulder and my whereabouts for the last ten years made me wish I had printed out index cards and handed them out as part of the badges everyone wore when they registered at the front table. Not that there was anyone I didn't recognize. Few people had changed much in ten years.

My answer, though, was always the same. "I blew out my shoulder and the docs thought it inadvisable to continue playing. My throwing would never be the same, not the range, the accuracy, or the length of time I could throw in a game. So I switched gears."

Then came the murmurs of sympathy followed by the "I really thought you were going to go all the way. Put us on the map. You were the champ, Bigs."

As if football was all that mattered. But to some of these people, it was. We had gone to the state championship, and we were all special for that one moment in time.

Of course, then came the other awkward questions. "What about you and Sadie? I thought you two were going to be the ones who made it. Are you together again?"

I didn't know how to answer that question. Yes, everyone thought we were the golden couple, who should have married after college and be on kid number two or three by now. Instead, I was still trying to get her to talk to me most days. At least she was here as my date. That was progress, right?

"Sadie is only with you out of pity, you know that, Bigsly. When you leave, and we all know you will, I'll be here to pick up the pieces. I've done it before, and I'll do it again." Paxton's smug face had me seeing red. Even the rest of the football team took a collective step back, as if sensing a potential fight.

I fisted my hands at my sides and counted to ten, telling myself the blowhard wasn't worth it. Before I could finish the second count of ten, a cool hand tucked under the crook of my elbow.

"Gentlemen. And Devon. Am I interrupting anything?"

I almost burst out laughing but settled for a smirk. With one cool cut, Sadie had defused the tension and managed to slam Paxton, cutting him down to the weasel he was. The tension leached out of everyone in an instant. Paxton snarled and stomped over to the bar. I gave a subtle throat cut to the bartender. Paxton had clearly had been indulging before he arrived, and I'd personally seen him have four whiskeys. He didn't need any more. He didn't like the bartender refusing to serve him, but before he could say anything, a couple friends of his ponied up to the bar and distracted him, leading him to the buffet and some food to soak up the booze in his stomach.

With that crisis averted, I turned my attention to more pleasurable pursuits. Everyone had drifted away now that the drama had been deflected, leaving Sadie and me alone. "How about you show me that water wheel up close and personal, Jax?"

Since she'd already seen it, I couldn't help but wonder if she needed some fresh air, much like I did. We headed out into the dusk, the light illuminating the darkness and the stone walkway to the water wheel. When we got there, she dropped my arm and stepped closer, as if inspecting the wood.

Without turning, she spoke. "You never answered my question."

"I didn't think we wanted an audience for it."

"We're alone now."

I nodded, my hands plunged into the pockets of my Dockers. "We are. Is that what you really want to talk about? The past?"

She took a deep breath and turned, her hazel eyes focused on me. "I know I should. I want to know what went wrong all those years ago. I thought everything was good between us. I thought we were solid, had good communication, had a plan. Then one day, it all fell apart."

I took a step forward, but I didn't reach for her. "What would it take for you to believe that it had nothing to do with you, that it was all me?"

I turned and took a few steps away, listening to the music from the reunion, the murmur of voices that drifted on the night sky. "The truth was it was all of that. All of them. I couldn't deal with the pressure, Sadie. Everyone expected so damn much of me, of us to be honest, but mostly me. No matter what I did, it was never enough. Regional champions? Great, how about state? Now how about college football, then professional, then on and on. When would it stop? I felt like I had the expectations of the whole town on my shoulders and what the hell did I do to deserve it? I threw a goddamn football well."

I whirled around and kicked a rock. It flew and hit the river that flowed past with a solid thunk. I stared out at the river in the darkness beyond. "And no matter what I said, it didn't matter. Teams win championships. We had the perfect storm of great players that year that worked well together. Was I a good quarterback? Sure. Could I make it at college or pro? Who knows? Maybe."

"But no one ever asked you if that was what you wanted." Her voice was soft, quiet, but I heard it nonetheless. It broke through the red haze of my anger and frustration.

My shoulders slumped, all anger drained out of me in that instant. "Yeah. Everyone just expected that I would do that. Then come back to Holly Creek and put them on the map, whatever that meant."

I felt a hand on my back. Sadie. Soothing me, stroking me, trying to take away my pain, like she always did. "Why didn't you tell me?"

I closed my eyes. "You loved it here. How could I tell you that Holly Creek was my problem, at least for a while? I needed a break, needed to get away and find who I was without this town and their expectations. I needed to find my way before I could figure out what I wanted to do next."

"I could have come with you," she said, her voice small and quiet.

I turned, pulling her close before she could step back. "No, Sadie. You had your plans, your own life to live. You didn't need to be burdened by my bullshit. You dealt enough with it that freshman year after my injury. I was terrible to you, and I'm sorry. I drove you away. I drove everyone away that first year."

She bowed her head. She knew I spoke the truth. I had been a real bastard that first year, dealing with the injury, the rehab and the pain, the frustrations, the unknown. Sadie had stuck by my side through all of it, trying to be the supportive girlfriend. Even then, I think I knew I had to leave and was trying to make it easier. If I was a bastard, she might break up with me or be relieved when I walked. But she wasn't. She hadn't understood. Had been devastated. I'd broken the final bond.

She swallowed hard. "I won't say it's okay because it's not. You were a bastard. But I understand why you did it. In fact, it may have been for the best. Were either of us really ready to truly commit to each other back then? Doubtful. We were a high school couple. What did we know of love, of life, of anything, really?"

My heart froze in my chest, and my stomach sank. Dammit. I was losing her. Sadie had brought me out here to break up with me, for good this time. She had her answer, the whole gut-wrenching truth, and now she was done with me. I deserved it, after all. I hadn't done anything to earn her love. She deserved so much more.

I steeled myself for the words, dropping my hands from her shoulders. "I understand. But please, don't date Paxton. Anyone but him. I couldn't take it."

A smile curved her lips, and she chuckled. "God, that was a mistake. I went out with him once or twice back when we first broke up. He's horrible. What makes you think I would ever go out with him again?"

Relief flooded me. At least I wouldn't have to see them date, hear Paxton crow about how he had Sadie now.

She stepped closer, her hands cupping my cheeks, forcing

me to look at her. "I'm done living in the past, Jax. I think it's time for me to start a new life. Do you want to be a part of it?"

Hope was kindled. "Are you asking me what I think you are?"

"Take me to bed, Jaxon. Make me yours. Again."

CHAPTER NINETEEN

SADIE

Unfortunately, we weren't able to escape so easily or quickly. Jaxon was still on call for the venue, and we had many people to get through before we got to the exit. Since his brewery was hosting the reunion, and he hadn't hired an event coordinator, he was on the hook for the night. I wouldn't abandon him, so I hung around and caught up with all my high school friends. And for some reason, I entered my friend Courtney Maddux's giveaway for a photo shoot. Specifically, for a boudoir photo shoot, though not to be confused with her stranger-boudoir shoots.

Naturally, I won. Because a boudoir photo shoot is the last thing I want to do. But when my name was announced as the winner, and I caught Jaxon eying me speculatively, I couldn't help but wonder if he'd be up for doing it with me. A rush of heat flooded me at the thought, and I suddenly couldn't wait for this night to be over so the real celebration could begin. Jaxon shot heated glances at me all night, keeping the heat between us on simmer, just waiting for the right moment. A casual touch here, a brief fleeting kiss there. My body was burning by the time the evening ended.

Finally, everyone cleared out, and the cleanup committee was done. Jaxon turned off the lights and tugged me to him, one arm wrapped around my waist. "Are you sure about this, Sadie?"

I pressed my lips to his for a brief moment, not letting the flames flare out of control. "I've never been more sure of anything. Take me home."

He swallowed hard, his fingers flexing against the flesh of my ass. "I have a roommate, my business partner, Sean. It might be best if we go to your place."

"Good thing I stocked up on supplies."

He arched an eyebrow, then tugged me out the door, locking up behind us. He drove carefully, deliberately to my house, focused on the drive, a muscle flexing in his cheek, the only sign of the tension riding him hard. I smirked to myself but didn't dare tease him. It had been a long time for me, and I was barely hanging by a thread.

As soon as we stepped through the doorway of my home, the heat of Jaxon's presence overwhelmed me. The electricity between us was palpable, like a brilliant starlight visible in broad daylight. I could feel the intensity of his gaze, my skin tingling with anticipation as I took him in.

He looked exactly the same as the last time I'd seen him, yet somehow also wholly different. His intense blue eyes were still the same, as were his ruggedly handsome features; but his demeanor, the way he carried himself, was somehow different. He was more confident, more in control of himself and of the situation. I felt my heart swell with desire at the sight of him, my body responding to his presence in a way I could not ignore.

"Hey," he said in a low voice, his eyes smoldering.

"Hey," I replied, suddenly shy.

He stepped closer and lifted a hand, his fingertips tracing lightly along the side of my face. I shivered in response, and his lips curved up into a small smile. We stood there like that for a moment, suspended in time, and the tension between us rose up like a live wire.

Breaking the spell, I stepped away and tugged him after me, leading him to the bedroom. Electricity sparked between us, sending tingles of sexual awareness through my body. I led him up the stairs, my heart racing with anticipation as I wondered what would happen next.

When we arrived in my bedroom, I wondered what he'd think of the space. The room was painted beige with coral accents on the headboard, pillows, accent rugs, and the facing on the bureau and end tables. The trim and bedsheets were white and seemed to shimmer in the light of the full moon. My bed stood in the center, the duvet soft and inviting. Thank God I'd cleaned my room before I left for the evening.

Jaxon looked around, his eyes darting over the furniture and furnishings before finally alighting back to me. His gaze was full of hunger and longing, and I felt a thrill run through me as I met his gaze. Taking a hesitant step closer, I shivered as a spark of electricity passed between us.

He reached out and pulled me in, our bodies colliding in an embrace that seemed more passionate than anything I'd ever experienced before. His lips found mine in a kiss that both soothed and aroused me, and I moaned into his mouth as we explored each other's lips.

His hands moved over my curves with a skillful precision that made my body ache for more. His fingertips sent trails of fire over my skin as he explored every inch of me, igniting something deep inside of me. He moved lower until he was cupping my buttocks with both hands, squeezing gently to let me know just how much he wanted me.

I gasped against his mouth as his tongue drove deeper into mine, exploring every corner of my mouth with an intensity that sent shivers down my spine. We stayed like that for what felt like an eternity, lost in each other, until finally he pulled away with a satisfied grin on his face.

His lips left my mouth eagerly as they trailed down my neck, each kiss evoking electric jolts of pleasure through my body. His hands moved over me with an assuredness that had me quivering in anticipation. Tearing off his shirt, I ran my hands over his taut muscles, tracing the definition of his chest and abdomen with hungry fingers. I felt a fire ignited inside me, stoked by every inch of him.

He clasped me, his eyes searing into mine. Then he threw me down onto the bed, and I could feel the heat emanating from his body as it hovered over me. He stared down at me with an insatiable hunger that threatened to consume me whole, and my heart raced as I felt myself giving in to him completely.

His lips crashed against mine in a passionate embrace, and I felt my whole body quivering as his hand moved slowly down it. His fingers trailed over me like fire, leaving a burning path of pleasure wherever they touched. I was lost in bliss, sensations so powerful that I thought I might burst into flames. As his touch grew more urgent, I clutched at him desperately, surrendering completely to his desire.

He pulled me close, crushing his lips on mine as our tongues intertwined and our bodies melted together like burning wax. I ran my hands over his toned muscles, feeling them flex beneath my fingertips. He moved his grip to my hips, pulling me closer as I opened myself up for him. His hardness pressed against my delicate skin with a powerful desire that threatened to overwhelm me.

The air tightened around us as I looked into his eyes. His gaze was like a laser, piercing me to my core and making me feel alive with a thousand butterflies. He moved closer until our lips were almost touching, then he pressed them softly against mine while whispering into my ear. "You're so fucking beautiful," he said, emotion thick in his voice.

At that moment, the world melted away. Our rhythm was all that mattered now, our love filling the air with a palpable energy. His hips rocked against mine in an intuitive dance, and I gasped as he entered me. The pleasure was like lightning coursing through my veins, building until it exploded into a crescendo of sensation.

My hips thrashed against his, a feverish passion radiating from me. His breathing grew heavy as I felt the strength of his longing course through him, quickly escalating to a wild frenzy. We moved together in an unyielding rhythm, becoming one with each other as our exhilaration peaked and we soared over the brink of pleasure together.

As we lay there, our bodies intertwined in the afterglow of our lovemaking, I felt a deep sense of connection between us. I knew that this wasn't just a physical connection, but an emotional one as well. I had found my true love—again—and I never wanted to let him go.

CHAPTER TWENTY

JAXON

I couldn't believe I was lying here in Sadie Taylor's bed. This wasn't the first time we'd slept together, but it felt like something new, like something had fundamentally changed between us. Maybe because we were both older, had grown up and become different people. This no longer felt the same as before. It felt more real, more concrete, more intense. My feelings for Sadie had deepened and grown into something I hadn't expected and, frankly, it was a little scary, especially since I didn't know what she was feeling.

She shifted in her sleep. Her hand, that had been still on my chest, began stroking me as if soothing me. "You're thinking awfully hard there. Regrets?"

"Definitely not."

I felt her lips curve into a smile against my shoulder. "Thinking about round two?"

"Definitely."

She lifted her head and propped her chin on my bicep. "And what else? Seriously, Jax. I can almost smell your brain burning cells."

I sighed and let my hand run over her hair, silky and smooth. "Just thinking about high school and how innocent our feelings were back then."

She arched an eyebrow and chuckled huskily. "I seem to recall several not so innocent feelings back then, and actions."

Damn, my cock was definitely rising to the occasion, thinking back to the swimming hole outside of Holly Creek, my dorm room, the makeout point. "No, you're right. We weren't all so sweet back then, but it seems so small compared to now."

Her brow furrowed. "What are you saying?"

Damn, this was harder than I thought it would be. It was so much easier in the heat of the moment. But I wasn't sure Sadie had heard me or even believed me. And I found I wanted—no, needed her to hear those words again, to believe me.

I shifted until I was half reclined on the bed, propped against the coral headboard. She repositioned herself to continue watching me warily, as if I was going to say or do something to hurt her. "Sadie, I care about you so fucking much. I always have, but I think it's something more now, beyond what I felt back when we were together. I regret everything that I did, how I hurt you, but now I think it may have been for the best, because now we are older and are more mature."

Her eyes had darkened during my words, and I wondered if I had pissed her off. But then she sighed. "I feel the same way too, Jaxon. I forgive you for leaving the way you did. I think you're right. We were too young to think we were ready for anything more. I regret how it all happened, but not how my life played out. Let's focus on the future."

I let out a breath that I hadn't even been aware that I had been holding. Then I gave her a wicked grin and rolled, reversing our positions so I was over her, settled between her thighs, my mouth an inch above hers.

"Ready for round two?"

She chuckled and closed the distance between us, rubbing herself against my erection. I groaned and sank into her, into the moment, and showed her how much I loved her.

CHAPTER TWENTY-ONE

SADIE

We spent Sunday in bed, only taking a break for food and the resulting conversation. The brewery gift shop and tasting room were open, but Jaxon had staff for that. Clara was handling the shop for me, since I was only open a few hours in the afternoon for summer tourists who came through the town. So we had the day to ourselves. Normally, we both would have been in our businesses, but we played hooky. And it was glorious.

It had been a long time since I'd had a reason to play hooky. I'd spent most of the last several years either working or focused on my business, so it seemed strange to have something else on my mind. When Monday rolled around and Jaxon left my house, I used the morning hours to work on a new recipe for my friend Chelsea's wedding favors. Today, I was focusing on raspberry and buttercream filled petit fours. I was trying to make them light, not too sweet, and refreshing. I wanted to send an assortment of options to Chelsea in New York City with her mom so she could tell me her thoughts.

"You got laid." Clara's voice broke into my focus, shattering the bubble I had been working in.

I glanced up with a curse after screwing up the delicate gold leaf decoration on top of the petit four. "How the hell would you know that? And thanks for messing me up."

She stared at me as if I was a seven-foot-tall, blue-skinned alien from one of her sexy romances. "Nope, you totally did. I can tell. You're smiling, humming, and buzzing around here like a busy little bee. No stomping, grunting, or general bad mood. I like it."

I straightened and pinned her with a look. "Have I really been that insufferable?"

Clara softened and slid onto the stool, swiping a petit four in the process. "No, you've just been really unhappy. I hadn't realized how much until right now. I take it the reunion was a success?"

My face burned hot, but before I could reply, the back door banged open, and Lila burst in, followed quickly by Courtney. Lila immediately searched my face, then gave a whoop. "I knew it! I saw you and Jaxon on Saturday night, and it was so obvious. You did the deed!"

I buried my face in my hands. "Oh my God, Lila. Just announce it to everyone in Holly Creek, why don't you?"

Courtney hugged me. "Good for you, Sadie. So, imagine what you could do with that boudoir shoot now?"

Three heads swiveled to stare at me, jaws dropping. "You won the photo shoot?" Lila screeched.

I sat heavily on the stool. "I did."

I still didn't know why I entered, and I had no idea if I could actually go through with it.

"What's that look for?" Courtney asked, as if she could guess where my mind had already wandered to. "You aren't going to chicken out on me, are you?"

Courtney was a kickass photographer who made fucking magic through the lens of a camera. Her photos were sexy, but also tasteful. They were gorgeous! A person would have to be an idiot to turn down a session with her. And yeah, I'd initially planned on tucking my prize away and conveniently forgetting about it. Nothing about my curvy body was anything I wanted plastered on a camera screen. But after the weekend with Jaxon, during which he had worshipped all parts of me without missing a beat, I was feeling empowered. I just didn't know if I should coax Jaxon into doing the shoot with me or if I should do it alone and give him a picture. Or if I would have the guts to do it at all!

I shook my head, refusing to walk away from this opportunity. "I'm trying to figure out when I can do it and if I want to do it alone."

Lila clapped her hands over her ears while the other two women cheered. "Nope, I do not want to think or hear about my brother doing a naked photo shoot."

Courtney peered over her nose at Lila. "They wouldn't be naked. What I do is very tasteful, and they're dressed. Mostly." She grinned before turning back to me. "I'd love to do whatever kind of shoot you'd like, Sadie. Whatever makes you most comfortable."

The idea of me and Jaxon together was growing on me and, frankly, turning me on. And having a picture remembrance of it would be hella sexy. Would Jaxon be up for it?

❄

I hadn't had a chance to bring up the photo shoot with Jaxon all week since we both were busy. Jaxon had the grand reopening on Labor Day weekend, and I was helping him where I could, while maintaining the shop. It was still tourist season in Holly Creek, the last week of the summer, so we were still fairly busy, and stock needed replenishing for the shop. Jaxon and I spent our evenings together, and it was nice to have someone to come home to, to eat dinner with, to talk to. I hadn't realized how lonely I had been until someone was around at night.

But the grand reopening of Tap Meister went off without a hitch, or none that I could see. Most of the town came out on Labor Day to celebrate the opening, with picnics on the lawn, music from the local band, and beer from the brewery, including a new brew just for the fall. Harvest Hues Amber Ale. It was clearly a hit as the crew in the tasting room was kept busy pouring mug of mug of it. I even had some, and it was delicious.

I was standing on the side watching Jaxon chat with some of the local businesspeople when I felt someone come up beside me. I turned to see Jaxon's father there. He was only in his sixties but appeared older, a little stooped, brown hair almost completely gray now, and his face heavily lined from a lifetime of frowns and disappointment.

"So you and my boy have taken up again. Do you think you can keep him this time and not drive him away?"

Jaxon's worried glance from across the stone patio noted his father with me, and I gave him a smile to cover my surprise at the blunt question.

"I wasn't the one who drove him away, Mr. Bigsly. Jaxon is an adult and made his own choices, and I respect them."

He grunted. "Not by the way you moped around here for so long. He won't stay, you know. This town is too small for him. He was always destined for bigger things, if only he wasn't held back."

I fully turned and faced the man who I realized had become even more bitter than I had over the way Jaxon had left, and it made me sad. "Are you implying that I held him, am still holding him back?"

"He's here for you. What do you think?"

"He's here to open Tap Meister. I would think that would make you happy. Didn't you work there for most of your life?"

He grunted again. "My son could have had a great life, been

somebody. And yet here he is back in this nothing town. He'll regret it. Wait and see. Then he'll hightail it out of here faster than you can say stay. Don't get attached. He'll only disappoint you."

I wanted to pass his words off as the ramblings of a bitter, angry old man. A father who was angry that his son hadn't lived up to the football dream that I knew he'd had for his son. But his warning spoke to the fear that lurked in my heart, the fear that Jaxon would wake up one day and wonder why the hell he was in Holly Creek when once before he couldn't wait to leave. Would he stay or would he go? And if he had no choice but to stay, tied to a family or something, would he grow to resent a wife or, God forbid, a child?

"Dad, what are you talking with Sadie about?" Jaxon's smile was firmly on his face, but it was anything but pleasant, as if he has known the conversation had taken a dark turn.

His father seemed to sense the same thing. "I was just warning your girl here about your tendency to roam. Isn't that what you do? Leave after a while, when you get bored or uncomfortable?"

Jaxon's smile faded, and a hard look entered his eyes. "I have moved around a bit since leaving college, but I was gaining work experience to be ready to take over Tap Meister. I'm ready to settle down. I know what I want and where I want to be."

His dad only made a noise and moved off with a last look at us, clearly not satisfied but unwilling to continue the conversation. Jaxon glared after him until he was gone from sight. Then he turned to me, tugging me off to the side and leaning in.

"You know he's full of shit, right? He is bitter and cranky and unhappy."

I sighed. "Your dad has always been unhappy. But he loves you. I think he missed you when you didn't come home."

"No, he was pissed that I didn't follow his plan for me. College football, the NFL, fame and glory. All for him."

I hugged Jaxon, feeling the tension in his body slowly leach out of him. He clung to me, resting his head on top of mine. "He's afraid to lose you."

Just like I am, I thought to myself, but I didn't dare add it. I wanted to believe he would stay. He'd bought a business here. If that didn't mean roots, what would?

He shuddered in my arms and lifted his head. "Well, he has a funny way of showing it. Are you ready to head out?"

"Sure. Hey, have you looked had a chance to look at the listings I sent you? I don't want to push but you mentioned having trouble finding something." My voice drifted off. I really didn't want to mention it but I wondered if he was staying, being as he was essentially renting a room from his business partner.

He grinned. "Tired of me hanging out at your place all the time? We can go to my place. Sean isn't home right now."

I shuddered. "No thanks. I like the comfort of my home."

He hugged me close. "I like it too. Your place feels like a home. We're still settling in." He sighed. "Holly Creek is a small town, and there aren't a lot of options, something I should have remembered, especially with the tight housing market. Sean found a rental with a couple of bedrooms and said I could crash there. I could never stay with my dad, and I wouldn't impose on Lila. And a hotel or the bed-and-breakfast wouldn't work. So I'm still looking for something."

A little warning bell flickered in my brain, but I ignored it. He'd find something permanent. Then he'd settle. This was a temporary situation. It wasn't because he didn't think he'd stay.

"You probably don't want to deal with Devon for your housing search," I teased.

Jaxon gave me a look of sheer horror. "He'd only show me the worst of the lot. No thanks. I'll check listings out as I see them."

I frowned, bothered by his nonchalance. "Jaxon, that's not the best way to go about it. You should get an agent and let them do the work. You're too busy for this. Let me call Nancy Sloane. She's amazing. No connection to Devon. In fact, she's great and a direct competitor. It'll burn his ass if you use her."

"Double win." He grinned. "Maybe. Let me get through the next few weeks and I'll call her."

He wrapped an arm around my shoulder and escorted me over to a table to talk to some people. I stuffed that warning bell deep inside, but it still resonated. *Be careful, Sadie Taylor. Be on alert.*

CHAPTER TWENTY-TWO

JAXON

Opening Day had been amazing. I sat at the table in the middle of the tasting room, my laptop open, and scanned through the pictures Sadie's friend Courtney had taken of the event, trying to pick the best ones that we could use for social media. She had even taken some of our working area for our website and brochures. She was brilliant, capturing the best angles and the beauty of the brewery, the unique history of the building and the modern touches. I couldn't help but wonder how her pictures of Sadie would be for the boudoir shoot.

My pants grew tight as I thought of Sadie in sexy lingerie, or less, in a boudoir photo shoot, and I groaned. I had hoped she would ask me to do a couples' shoot with her, but she hadn't said anything. I knew she was self-conscious, since she talked about being more curvy than other women, but I loved her curves. I hope she knew that, especially since I took extra time to show her every night. I hoped I got to see the result of the shoot, as long as she went through with it.

My phone buzzed, and I checked my text messages. Sadie, with a contact card. Nancy Sloane, the realtor. I felt guilty about ducking Sadie's conversation about finding a place. I hadn't wanted to admit that I wasn't ready to find my own place, not yet, not when I might get the internship in Germany. I could always find a place when I got back. But I couldn't tell Sadie why.

My phone buzzed again, and I almost ignored it, but reflexes had me checking and it was Sean. He'd planned to make it to Holly Creek for the opening, but a flight cancellation had him stuck in Houston. With the final days of wrapping up his prior consulting work, as well as two meetings later in the week with distributors we were anxious to land, he'd given up on the weekend to focus on the coming days.

I tapped to answer the call, and Sean's voice came through. "Hey, the pictures look great from the opening. Who was the photographer?"

"A friend of Sadie's. They're great. Will be great on the website too."

"And with some of the PR stuff I'm working on. Send me her info so I can make sure she gets photo credit."

"Will do." We talked about the opening for a moment, and I knew Sean was looking forward to being in Holly Creek full time. He would be there for good by the end of the week. I paused before asking, "Do you mind me staying with you?"

"What? Of course not. The house is plenty big enough. Why? Have you found a place?"

"I haven't started looking yet," I admitted.

"I thought you were going to wait until you heard about the internship in Germany. It wouldn't make sense to rent a place, then be gone for six months if you got it. Has anything changed?"

"No, I'm still waiting to hear. Sadie just asked me about finding a place and I wondered if you were still okay with me crashing at your place. That's all."

"Absolutely okay. Stay as long as you want—even if you

don't get the internship. You haven't told Sadie about that possibility, then?"

Shit, no I hadn't. I had been so focused on convincing her to give me a shot, that I wasn't going anywhere, that I hadn't wanted to muddy the waters with the potential opportunity in Germany. Sean, being the insightful business partner and friend that he was, saw right through my silence.

"Dude, you have to tell her. If she hears from anyone else, she's going to be pissed."

"Why would she be pissed? It's a career opportunity, and I'll only be gone six months. I'll be coming right home. I have a business here. It's not like I won't be back."

"Right. But are you sure you want to keep this from her?"

Damn it. I hated it when Sean was right. "Someday, I'm going to be your voice of reason, and you'll hate me for it."

I could almost hear the shrug in his voice. "Maybe. Let's talk Oktoberfest. And winter ale."

Finally, a subject I was comfortable with. "I want to make a chocolate stout for the holiday season. I've been experimenting, and I think I have the right recipe."

"Inspired by your girlfriend?" Sean teased.

Sadie made everything better. So why was I keeping secrets?

❄

I waited until things settled after the grand opening to approach Sadie about my idea. With her palate, I wanted her to help me taste test the batch I was working on and get her advice on the recipe I was perfecting. I was close on the recipe, but she might have some suggestions for me, though I had wanted the beer to be a surprise for her.

We were having dinner at her place and had finished the Chinese food when I pulled out my notebook and the six-pack from previous years' attempts at a milk stout, the base I wanted to use for this recipe. Sadie arched her eyebrow.

"You know I'm not a beer fan, right? Wine is more my style. Beer is often so bitter." She wrinkled her nose as she spoke.

I snorted. "You haven't had the right beer. No, I need your help with my Christmas beer. I've been working on a milk stout, and I think I figured out a way to make it unique. Add chocolate to it."

Her eyes widened. "You can add chocolate to beer? Like melt down some candy and mix it in? Or would you use powders or cacao beans?"

"Actually, there are a lot of ways we could do it, and I've tested a few already in small batches. Did you know that most chocolate beers are really made with a chocolate malt, which is a malted barley and not chocolate at all? It adds what people call chocolate-like aroma and taste, but it's not really chocolate."

Sadie frowned. "That seems like cheating."

I shrugged, flipping through the pages of my notebook that doubled as a recipe book. "Maybe, but chocolate is hard to work with. It comes in so many forms, so you have to decide where best to add it to the process. There are so many points, and it affects the end result differently."

"Brewing beer is a lot like cooking. A lot of trial and error."

"Yup, except you have a wait a few weeks to test your product and take really detailed notes on what you did to find out your results." I found the page. "Okay. So bars and cocoa powder aren't worth it. Chocolate malt, like I mentioned before, is the easiest, but I really want to get more real chocolate in this stout. I have the milk stout base down. I think adding a choco-late note to it would be amazing."

I opened one of the beers and poured a little in a glass. "Try this."

Sadie eyed it skeptically, but she picked it up and took a sip. Like a true taster, she let it linger on her palate, then swished in it in her mouth before swallowing. Her eyes went wide, and she smiled. "Jaxon, that's delicious. A little sweet, not at all bitter like I expected."

"The lactose cuts some of the bitter of the stout, making it smoother. Imagine it with a hint of chocolate now."

"Or even strawberries. That would be amazing." Her excitement was growing, and I was feeding on it.

"Exactly! I have a couple of options to try, but I don't really have time to test now. I have to pull the trigger because we can either play it safe, make this stout and go easy this holiday season, or go big and try for something truly great."

She grinned. "You want to go deep, like you did in the championship game when you were down by five and had only two minutes in the game."

My heart pounded in my chest. "Exactly. I've been preparing for this moment. I know this recipe is the right one."

"So what do you need me for?"

I rubbed my jaw with my hand. "I wanted to run my ideas by you, see if what I was thinking about the chocolate made sense during the brewing process. You understand chocolate. You might have some thoughts."

Her cheeks turned pink. "You want my help? I don't know much about brewing beer, but I'll do what I can."

"But you know chocolate. Okay, so, I'm leaning toward using roasted cocoa nibs, along with chocolate malt in the beer. Everything else seems to create a problem in the process."

"May I look at your notes?"

I handed over my notebook, and we spent the next few hours reviewing the notes, talking through the brewing process and what I had already tried in my smaller test batches, and how the different forms of chocolate had taken to the process. Most of them had not gone well, frankly. Some were downright disastrous.

Sadie then pulled out her laptop and tapped away, doing

some of her own research. It was late when we finally hammered out a recipe that we both felt would work.

"Are you sure you don't want to run a test on this first?"

I shook my head. "It's already September. I'm late for a holiday beer. I need this ready to ship by the end of November at the latest."

She reached across the table and gripped my hand. "Jax, this isn't the state championship. You have more than two minutes. You have a lifetime."

Maybe I did, but I had a possible internship that could call any day, and I would be leaving for six months. I had to leave Tap Meister with several recipes ready to brew so we could start on a firm foundation. Jed had cut way back on production, not making anything new in years and sticking with his familiar beers. Those were fine, but a brewery couldn't survive by being stagnant. Sean and I needed to show that we were growing and were worth taking a chance on for the distributors, the bars, and the shops, starting regionally then hopefully spreading out. To do that, we needed fresh beer in the bottles.

Now would be the perfect time to explain all of that to Sadie, to let her know I had my last step in my brewing mastery within my grasp. This internship would give me that final notch and solidify my status as a brewmaster. If I got it, that is.

But I kept my mouth shut. "I know. I'm still trying to prove myself to everyone. Put Holly Creek on the map."

I laughed it off and hoped she wouldn't ask anything else.

I closed my notebook and gave her a side-eyed look. "Now how about we celebrate?"

A smile teased her lips, but she held it back. "Shouldn't we wait until you taste it?"

I wouldn't be here to taste it, if everything worked out like I hoped. My assistant would run everything in my absence. I stuffed that thought deep inside a box and shoved a lid on it. "So we have two times to celebrate."

I got to my feet and walked around the table, pulling her to me. She wound her hands around my neck. "What did you have in mind? Want to go for ice cream?"

"I want a treat, all right, but I think I'll stay in for it."

She chuckled as I lowered my head and claimed my prize.

CHAPTER TWENTY-THREE

SADIE

September flew by. Between planning for Oktoberfest, continued testing of chocolates for Chelsea's wedding, though we were getting close there, and nights spent with Jaxon, I was busier than ever. But I also had never been happier. I hadn't realized how quiet my life had gotten or how lonely it was before he had come home. While Jaxon still technically lived with his business partner, he spent most nights at my house. He hadn't started looking for his own place, and I wondered if he was dragging his feet because he was hoping for us to move in together. Jaxon had never been one to linger over a plan. If he saw something he wanted, he went out and got it. I tried not to dwell on it, because it only made that little voice in my head louder, and I was ignoring it. Things were good between us, and I didn't want to screw it up.

Though, how I got here was still a mystery.

I was standing in the boudoir section of Courtney's studio, the downstairs back living space of an historic house she'd purchased several months before. The house set back off the road and had a yard full of trees, providing plenty of privacy for her customers. There was a bedroom area set up on one side of the room, as well as a small kitchen section, a stand-alone tub with a modern, freestanding faucet in one corner, and a handful of uniquely shaped chairs, all covered in rich luxurious fabrics. What I could only assume to be props for the photo shoots were stored on a large set of shelves, with what appeared to be movable backgrounds slid in behind the shelves. One of the backgrounds was even a large mirror.

I turned in a circle, alone in the room for the moment, taking it all in. The sheer drapes over the floor-to-ceiling windows were parted just enough that the early afternoon sunlight winked through the opening, slicing a path across the original hardwood flooring, and for some reason, I found myself wanting to slide one foot forward until my toes reached that glowing rectangle.

I took a sip of the wine Courtney had offered when I'd arrived and wondered what had gotten into me. It was as if I'd already stepped outside of my own body and were another person.

Courtney entered the room, coming around the corner from the hallway and tilted her head at me. A gentle smile curved her lips. "You about ready to get started?"

I gulped another drink and nodded. She'd talked me into doing a solo photo shoot before Jaxon arrived to help me get more comfortable in front of the camera. I told Jaxon I was coming early to help her with her Oktoberfest booth setup.

"Am I going to have to take off the robe?" I blurted out. I might have wanted to sensuously slide my toes into the sunlight only seconds before, but the nerves were still there.

"You don't have to do anything you don't want to, Sadie. This is your shoot. Your moment to be whatever you want to be. You can be fully dressed, you can stay as you are, you can wear whatever you want."

Courtney's soothing voice was calming me. A little. I turned my wineglass up yet again. I wore black lingerie under my very short robe, both purchased for this occasion, and I looked like some kind of sex goddess that had just rolled out of bed thanks to Sam doing my hair and makeup before I came over. I knew Courtney wouldn't judge me. She was awesome. But that damned camera…

"I will admit," Courtney continued as she fidgeted with the camera in her hand, "I am hoping you'll stick with the lingerie. Because you look fucking amazing. Jaxon is going to lose it when he sees you later."

I felt my face burning. "Really?"

"I wouldn't lie." She winked then said, "Give me one more minute then I'll be right back. You get to decide where we begin."

She disappeared the way she'd come, and I crossed to the corner where the bathtub stood. Nearby was a full-length, gold-framed mirror, and I peered at my reflection. I shrugged out of the robe. That wasn't doing it for me. Instead, I grabbed the bag of options Courtney suggested I bring and pulled out the men's button-down shirt I'd impulsively stuffed inside, the one Jaxon had left at my house. I buttoned that over my lingerie, leaving the top four buttons undone, and looked at myself once again. A fashion model I was not. But I felt good. I could do this. And strangely, I wanted to do this.

I chose the bed. I was here, so I wanted to go for it.

When Courtney returned, she took one look at me sitting with my back straight, barely positioned on the corner of the mattress, and nodded. Then we got started. For the first pose, all I did was stay where I was. Courtney directed me to bring my knees in together, one slightly higher than the other, and cross my arms over the top knee. I didn't smile, but I listened to every instruction and did the best I could. We transitioned from that to going to my knees, my feet tucked underneath me. I slipped Jaxon's shirt down over one of my shoulders, and Courtney's soothing voice showed me how to arch my neck backward, exposing my throat in just the right way. My fingers played with the ends of my hair. I dragged one fingertip down the middle of my bottom lip and on down, between my breasts.

Courtney took shot after shot as I switched positions, growing more comfortable with each new pose. After I stretched out and let the shirt slip from my body, arching my back up off the bed and sliding the fingers of one hand into my hair, I realized I'd closed my eyes when I heard the sound of the camera shutter clicking then Courtney making a little humming sound.

My eyes popped open. "What? Did I do it wrong? Do I look bad?"

Courtney grinned and turned the camera around so I could see the screen on the back.

"Oh my God. That's me?" I whispered. My hand went to my mouth. I still looked like the sex goddess Sam had made me into, only now I looked like one who knew she was a sex goddess. One proud of her body. I looked up at Courtney, my eyes wide. "What can we do next?"

Soft laughter came from Courtney, and by the time we'd finished with the shoot, I was more than ready to do the same with Jaxon.

*A*n hour later, I stepped from the studio changing room for the second time that day, this time wearing the thigh-high wool socks we'd ended our earlier session with, as well as the new lingerie and Jaxon's shirt. Jaxon was standing by window, overlooking the backyard and river that ran beyond it. He wore only his low-slung jeans, with the top of his boxers peeping out, and I was feeling hella jealous that even Courtney saw him like that.

He turned, and the look on his face made every bit of the

stress of the day worthwhile. Instant lust, desire, and heat slammed into me. "Sadie, holy shit. You look fucking amazing," he said thickly.

Courtney smirked as she fiddled with her camera. "Told ya. This is going to be so much fun."

We started by the windows, Jaxon cupping my cheek as Courtney suggested, and gazing into my eyes. His shirt was slipped over my shoulders, the raw lust in his eyes scorching me as he mesmerized me. He leaned forward, his lips a tantalizing inch from mine, ghosting over my skin. My head fell back, and he kissed down my throat with teasing kisses and nips, while his other arm was wrapped firmly around my back. He held my lower body against him, his erection pressing hot and heavy into my belly.

He reversed our positions, not waiting for further direction, pushing my hot body into the cool window, the changing in temperature doing nothing to cool my rising lust for him. He lifted me, and I wrapped my legs around his waist, his cock settling into the place it wanted to call home, but my lace panties were in the way. The shirt, still buttoned, draped around us. He kissed me as if his life depended on it, as if he was starving, and I buried my fingers in his hair, holding him to me, not letting him go.

We then moved to the chair where I straddled him and got some payback, teasing him by rocking back and forth on his cock, feeling my wetness soaking the panties and through to his low-slung jeans. I ran my nails down his chest, stroking his nipples, and he groaned. My head fell back, my hair loose, shook out behind me. He wound his fist in it and tugged me to him, claiming my lips in a deep, bruising kiss.

He surged to his feet and stumbled to the bed, tumbling me on my back into the center, following me down and caging me in place. He stared down at me for the longest time, as if memorizing my face.

"Sadie, I love you so fucking much."

Tears sprang in my eyes. I hadn't expected those words. Before I could speak, he pressed a finger to mine. "Shh. Not now. I just had to say it."

I wiggled and tried to get to the buttons. Interpreting my actions, he laid a hand on the shirt and gave me an inquiring look. I nodded, and he slipped the first button out, kissing the skin revealed. He then continued to undo each button, kissing his way down my torso until he spread the shirt out from my body, revealing the black lacy lingerie set.

"Goddamn it, Sadie. There is so much I want to do and having a camera here is so fucking inconvenient."

"Not to mention illegal," I quipped.

"Actually, not technically, but I don't do that kind of photography," Courtney piped up.

"But if I'm nearly naked," I tugged at his jeans, "these need to go."

He jumped off the bed, ready to strip the jeans off faster than a stripper's velcro pants, but Courtney's words halted him.

"Let's do a few with the jeans undone first. Jaxon standing, and Sadie on the bed, your fingers curled into the top of his boxers while you look up at him."

I swallowed, remembering that yes, we were there for a photo shoot. And based upon the shots Courtney let me see me earlier, these were going to be spectacular. So I obeyed. I lifted up, letting my back arch the way she'd taught me earlier, and positioned myself as she'd said. I could feel the tension in Jaxon's body as he stared down at me.

"Look at him as if you've been stranded on an unforgiving desert and he's the first glimpse of water you've had in days."

The click of the camera continued as my mouth went dry, and as we stared back at each other, my thought echoed Jaxon's earlier one. Too damned back there was someone else in the room because I was so ready to jump this man and fuck his brains out.

After several minutes, he was given the go-ahead to remove his jeans, and he climbed back on the bed and rolled us onto his back. If Courtney said anything else, neither of us heard it as Jaxon pulled me in for another deep, soul-stealing kiss, his hands buried in my hair. His hands roamed my body, stroking, teasing, taunting me with the possibilities, but not enough to send me over.

Then, in one sudden move, I was back on the bottom, and he got serious. He kissed his way down my body, still covering me mostly, but his hands traveled and dipped below my panties to trace my wet folds. I gasped, arching my back. He chuckled against my throat and stroked, alternating between dipping inside and circling my clit. My hips moved against him and I moaned, my hand clutching his shoulders, nailing digging into his skin. He sucked a little love bite at the top of my breast and pinched my clit, sending me screaming into an orgasm. He continued to stroke and soothe me until I had settled.

I slowly opened my eyes, dreamily staring at him. A camera click registered, and I arched on the bed. "Oh my God."

Courtney snickered. "That was a little more than I normally get out of my subjects, but damn, you two are the best I've had the honor to shoot. Thank you for letting me do this."

My face burned hot, but Jaxon kissed me and murmured, "there is no shame in pleasure, baby."

I hugged him to me. He was right. I loved him and he loved me. Oh wait!

"I love you, Jaxon."

The camera shutter clicked once more, memorializing that moment forever.

CHAPTER TWENTY-FOUR

JAXON

We stumbled through the door, barely making it over the threshold before we were tearing at our clothes. Sadie barely had her jeans off and I was on her, pressing her into the wall and kissing her like my life depended on it, the attraction sizzling between us. Our lips clashed, our tongues dueling, devouring each other like we were starved.

Her sultry lines and inviting curves that had been taunting me all day during the photo session filled my senses, sweeping away my worries and inspiring an urgent desire to be close to her. I leaned in and pinned Sadie against the door. The warmth from her body seeped into mine. I caged her lightly, striving for control. I didn't want to take her against the wall, but I was barely hanging on, my control shot from a day of teasing.

I moaned and moved my hands to her waist, and then up her back. Her body shuddered with pleasure, and her breathing grew heavy. My heart pounded in my chest, and a fire burned inside me. She was so fucking perfect in every way. Her lips were warm and inviting, and our kiss was electric, igniting an inferno of desire that raced through me and left me craving more.

My hands moved up her back and around her neck, plunging into her hair to angle her for my kiss. I trailed kisses over her face, cheeks, lips, jawline. Her head fell back with a moan, and she gripped my hair, her nails digging in with a prick of pain.

I moved one hand to her waist and the other to the back of her thigh, lifting it around me, opening her so I could settle between her legs, notching my aching cock where it longed to be. Her body trembled under my caress, and it was intoxicating. I trailed my fingers higher up her soft thigh, inching the long white shirt up as I went.

My other hand drifted to her chest, and then I ran my fingers down the plane of her chest. They glided across shallow dips and rises as they made their way to the fabric that covered her breasts. Her breath quickened at my touch, and her nipples pebbled against my hand.

She gasped, and her head fell back against the wall, arching her body into my touch. I tugged her shirt open, revealing the lace that had teased me throughout the photo shoot earlier that day, that black lace playing peekaboo with her soft skin. I tweaked one of her nipples through the lace, and she squealed.

"We should move upstairs," she murmured, her husky voice breaking the silence of the hallway.

"Not yet," I replied and bent to take her lips with mine again.

We kissed passionately, our mouths exploring one another's, our tongues playing and teasing each other. I moved my other hand back to her thigh and pulled it higher around my waist, rubbing my cock against her soft core. I was so hard and aching, my cock like an iron rod against the fly of my jeans pressing against her. I couldn't wait for the bedroom. I wanted her. I needed her now.

I lifted her other thigh, and she wrapped her legs around my waist. We kissed passionately, and I moved my hands to her hips, holding her close as I moved us. Without breaking the kiss, I stumbled into the living room and dropped her on the couch. I quickly stripped off the rest of my clothes, careful to grab the condoms from my pocket and sheathe myself.

Sadie tossed her white shirt and the lace underthings before I had a chance to stop her. She gave me a sultry smile. "What are you waiting for?"

I paused, just soaking in her beauty. Today's photo shoot had been incredibly stressful for her. She had been so self-conscious about her incredible curves, but she was fucking gorgeous, and I vowed to show her. Next time. Right now, I was too turned on to wait.

"You know you're beautiful, right? The most gorgeous woman ever."

Tears pricked her eyes, and she blinked rapidly to hold them back. "Jaxon, you don't have to say things like that. I'm kind of a sure thing."

I climbed onto the couch, kneeling above her. I took her chin in my hands and forced her to look at me. "No, I mean it. You've always been the most beautiful woman to me. Always. But it's not just your incredible body. You have an incredible heart, taking care of everyone, making sure that everyone is included and happy. And you're smart, starting your own business and always looking for ways to grow. You're everything, Sadie. I'm so fucking lucky that you forgave me and let me back in your life."

Now her tears were spilling down her cheeks, and I kissed them away. "I thought we weren't dwelling on the past. You're pretty awesome, too, you know. But right now, I don't care about the past."

I wedged myself between her thighs and kissed her long and deep. "The past is over. We're making our own future now."

She sank into the kiss, pulling me close. "A better one."

She wrapped her legs around my waist and arched her hips, sliding my cock against her core. She moaned, her eyes closing. "Definitely."

I kissed her slowly, exploring her mouth with my tongue, tasting her sweetness and her desire. I moved my hands around her body, feeling her warmth, her curves, her beauty. I kissed my way down her body, spending time on her glorious breasts, tweaking and teasing her nipples until she was writhing beneath me. I moved lower and lower, tasting everything I could, worshipping every inch of her until I reached her center, hearing her cries of pleasure grow louder.

She arched her back, but I held her firmly in place as I tasted her. I ran my tongue slowly over every inch of her core, from her opening up her clit. She moaned and writhed under me, trying to force me closer to her center. I took a moment to taste the little nub, flicking it lightly with the tip of my tongue before kissing all around it. Her cries filled my ears, growing louder as her pleasure grew. And then I slipped my fingers in her, massaging her gently. I felt her walls clench, as she exploded around me.

I moved up her body and kissed her neck, nipping it gently with my teeth. I slipped my cock into her, inch by inch, slowly pushing my way into her tight pussy. She arched her back, and her eyes rolled back in her head, and I knew she was lost to the feeling. She felt so good, so tight, and she felt even better as I moved in her. I thrust into her again and again, forcing her hips to the couch. I moved her body to my rhythm, sliding my cock in and out of her. Her moans grew louder, her breathing more labored, her body wrapped around me, writhing in pleasure. She wanted me. She wanted all of me. I wanted all of her.

I began fucking her in earnest. I thrust harder and deeper into her, and she was lost to her pleasure. Her breath grew heavier, and her body thrashed around beneath me, her moans growing louder and louder.

"Fuck yes," she moaned, her voice hoarse and breathless.

I took her legs and wrapped them around me, holding her body tight against mine as I thrust into her again and again, deeper and harder.

I focused on her body, the feel of her tightness and her warmth. I listened to her sounds, her moans, and the way she writhed under me. And I sank into the the way she felt, her body pressed against me. I was completely absorbed by everything about her, and it was intoxicating. I loved the way her body clamped down on my cock, the way her legs wrapped around me as her small hands gripped my back, nails digging into my skin. The way she arched her back. The way her beautiful body moved, like a dance. The way her skin glowed, her breath coming in rhythmic gasps. The way she moaned, ever increasing in urgency.

I held on to her tightly as I fucked her, and she held on to me, pulling me in closer, guiding me as she tried to force me deeper inside her. I thrust into her over and over; the moment growing more intense and hotter.

I gazed into her eyes, and she gazed into mine, and there was a connection, a moment of emotion that reached straight into our souls. It was more than just the moment we were sharing. It was a genuine connection, one I never wanted to sever.

Her eyes fluttered and her body tensed, and she cried out. Her body convulsed around me, a warm explosion of pleasure. Her legs squeezed me tightly, and her hands gripped my skin, nails digging into my back. My release built, held back by sheer willpower. Tension built in my body, and my muscles grew taut and my cock felt like it was ready to burst. I felt my release boil and spike as I erupted inside her, filling her with my seed. I kept thrusting lightly into her, and her body shook with another climax, and another, and another, as my cock twitched and pulsed inside her. Several minutes later, I collapsed beside her on the couch. She rolled over, laying her head on my chest. I kissed the top of her head and wrapped my arms around her. I held her close, feeling like I had finally come home.

Now I hoped I wouldn't fuck it all up.

CHAPTER TWENTY-FIVE

SADIE

Oktoberfest was in full swing, and I was beyond stressed out. It had been a week since my photo shoot and the most amazing weekend marathon of sex that I had ever had in my life. Granted, I had never had a marathon weekend of sex before, so I didn't have much to compare it to, but I couldn't imagine it getting any better. But since that weekend, I'd been too busy to do much more than text or chat on the phone with Jaxon. Both of us had been insanely busy preparing our businesses for the festival and setting up on the town green. I only really saw him at setup. And yet I wondered if I could take him behind one of the food tents for a quickie. It wouldn't take long. My body wasn't prepared to go a week with an orgasm. Not since Jaxon had come home.

"Oh, just grab him and have your way with him already. The longing looks are killing the rest of us. I'm kind of afraid you'll set the town green on fire," Clara laughed as she helped me with the tablecloth for our booth.

I blushed and refocused on the table. "I don't know what you mean."

"Bullshit," Courtney replied. "You should have seen their photo shoot. The hottest I've ever done. Hands down."

"Can we see the photos? Wait, no, that's my brother you're talking about. I really don't need to see that. But Sadie getting freaky? I kind of need to see that. Oh, this is hard," Lila moaned.

"That's what she said," Courtney snickered.

"All of you, stop it," I hissed as Jaxon strode over with a flyer in his hand.

"Sadie, you were serious about a wiener dog race?"

I laughed. "Yup, the brewery sponsors the trophy. I could swear I told you about it."

"You did, but I thought it was some kind of eating contest for hot dogs. Not a real wiener dog race."

I frowned. "I don't know how I could have been clearer. It's all in good fun. It's a short race to limit any injuries. It actually started with Jed when he had a dachshund. He loved that dog and took her everywhere. He saw a race online or somewhere and thought it would be fun. It's been a big draw, believe it or not. It's only been over the last seven or eight years, I think."

He shook his head. "Okay, if no one will get all cranky about it. It just seems weird. Our area is all set. I know you wanted to check it out. I'll meet you over there."

I smiled, conscious of the inquiring eyes studying us like we were a science experiment. Jaxon winked and walked away. All three of my former friends started fanning themselves.

"Damn, I thought we'd have to call the fire department. You do know that we're in a heightened state of fire danger since we haven't had any rain in a while, right?" Clara arched her eyebrow.

I rolled my eyes and finished smoothing the tablecloth. "It was all perfectly businesslike."

"Not the undertones. They said, *Come and check out my back room*." Lila made a swivel motion with her hips, then stopped. "Oh my God. That's my brother. I just can't. Not even for you."

Everyone laughed. Courtney then turned to me. "I'm sorry, Sadie, that I haven't gotten you the proofs. It's been a crazy this week. But seriously, the shots were amazing." Her tone lowered and she shifted her body more so only I could hear her next words. "Especially the photos that were of just you."

I hadn't yet told the other girls about the solo session we'd done. I took a half step back, and Courtney followed my movements, separating our conversation even more from the others.

"I have to admit," I told her, "I almost cancelled like a dozen times. But you made it so easy. And fun. Even when it was just me. I felt . . ." I shook my head, at a loss for what I'd felt. Sexy as hell, for sure. As much as when it had been both Jaxon and me in front of the camera.

All remaining traces of teasing were gone from Courtney's face. "I know. And I'm glad. What you're feeling right now, Sadie, that's my goal. Along with the fun and naughtiness that comes with a couple's shoot, I love helping women to realize their own beauty. To explore their sensuality. It thrills me every time I see a woman come out of her shell and take pride in the body she owns. To claim her womanhood."

I nodded. Yes, that exactly. Owning who I am as a woman. Being empowered by it. I stood a little taller. Who I am is a curvy, sexy, freaking hot-as-hell bombshell! Still...

I bit my lower lip. "You won't show them to anyone, will you?"

Courtney crossed her fingers over her heart. "No way. I'd ask you to sign a waiver if I ever wanted to use any for promotional or other reasons, but my guess is you wouldn't be comfortable with that, so I won't ask. The pictures are all yours. You won the prize, so I won't even share the couple's shots with Jaxon when they're ready."

I shook my head. "He has a right to those since he's in there, too. Share them with him. That's fine. But I might want to choose my own time to show him the ones with just me. Especially since he doesn't know I did it."

Courtney's smile returned. "You got it, gorgeous." She stepped back and included Lila and Clara as well. "Okay, I'm off. I've got to stop by my booth and check on my mother before I get busy being the 'official photographer of the festival.'" She grinned wider. "Make sure Mom isn't scheming to push work like what I recently did for Tap Meister at the grand opening. Because you know her, she's not the biggest fan of my stranger-boudoir shoots."

She tossed a wave and headed off, and Clara and Lila swiveled their attention back to me. "What was that all about? Why so private?"

"We uh . . ." I swallowed before blurting out, "were talking about the solo session I did before Jaxon showed up."

"What?" Both women screeched at the same time.

"You did a boudoir shoot, just you?" Clara added.

"Shhh." My heart rate had sped up, and my hands were now sweating. But I had to tell them about the shoot. I fucking loved it. I nodded and let the smile fill my face. "I did. And oh my gosh, it was amazing. The entire process was so painless. So exhilarating. Courtney isn't just a great photographer, she's a freaking genius. She's amazing, and I highly recommend doing a shoot like that yourself. " I gave Lila a sly look. "Tom might like something like that as a Christmas present."

Lila looked thoughtful as I headed off to deal with another disaster.

CHAPTER TWENTY-SIX

JAXON

"And you said we agreed to sponsor this?" Sean gave me a skeptical look as we stood at the finish line of the wiener dog race holding a weird gold statue with a dachshund on it. "And these outfits were part of the requirement?"

"Yup. Apparently it's tradition or something. Jed Turner had a dachshund and wanted to race her." Though the outfits were more of a suggestion than a requirement, not that I was going to tell Sean that.

We were dressed, as were our staff and the supplementary team that was serving in the Biergarten, in traditional Bavarian costumes, to lend authenticity to the entire experience. The women wore a dirndl dress, with tight, laced bodices in earthy tones, greens and browns, and sometimes heavily embroidered. They had white blouses underneath with puffed sleeves, but the entire outfit showed impressive cleavage. An apron finished the ensemble to signify they were working, separating them from the people who came just to cos-play, something I never knew people did for an Oktoberfest, but apparently, the Holly Creek people took Oktoberfest seriously. Sadie was dressed in traditional attire, her dirndl making her body look so damned sexy, and I was dying to show her how I appreciated it. I, on the other hand, looked like a little boy in short pants. She burst out laughing the first time she saw me. I hadn't gotten over the embarrassment.

Sean and I, on the other hand, wore traditional lederhosen with stripes across the top, something I didn't think he'd forgive or forget soon. We both wore the short leather breeches decorated with intricate embroidery and suspenders to hold them up, along with an embroidered leather band across our chest connecting the suspenders. We stayed plain for our shirts, both wearing white, tucked into the lederhosen. Knee-length socks, brown shoes, and wide leather belts completed the ensemble. We were twins, as befitting the new owners of Tap Meister. Sean was still fuming.

Sean turned a disbelieving look at me. "You know the dogs' legs are like three inches long. Racing can't be good for them." He tugged at the neck of the shirt. "The idea is as ridiculous as these outfits."

I shrugged. "I agree, but I didn't arrange it. I'm just going along with it. We can make our protests for next year, okay? For now, smile for the camera. It's good for business."

I wrapped an arm around Sean's shoulder and smiled at Sadie's friend Courtney, who had been running around all day snapping pictures of the festival. Sean's gaze caught on her for a long moment, then turned back to the race and chaos that ensued when they fired the starter pistol.

Some dogs ran. A couple cowered or turned and ran for their owner. And a couple more visited other dogs or people along the way. Chaos was a good way to describe it. Only one dog was taking it seriously, a pretty little dog who streaked for the end zone, her long ears flapping behind her, little legs pumping. Her owner picked her up and snuggled her.

Damn it. It was Jed. I sensed a ringer. When he pulled a treat out of his pocket, I was sure of it.

I nudged Sadie, who was standing a few feet away. "So how many years has Jed won?"

She looked uncomfortable. "All but two."

I scowled but quickly changed it to a smile when the crowd turned their attention to Sean and me for the presentation of the trophy. Once that was done, I looked for Sean, but he had disappeared.

I nudged Sadie. "Want to get something to eat? I hear the Biergarten is good this year."

She laughed, the sound making me warm inside. "Sorry. I promised Clara that I would give her a break at the booth. Maybe in a couple of hours."

"Sure." I kissed her, a deep kiss that left no doubt to her or anyone who watched that she was mine. She clung to me for a long moment, then broke away. Her eyes were a little dazed and unfocused, and she stumbled a bit before righting herself and walking away.

"I like her," Sean said as he reappeared by my side, an over-sized pretzel in hand. "Does she know?"

I sighed and fingered my phone in my pocket. "I only just found out this morning."

"You accepted, though, right?"

"Yeah. I talked to them and accepted the internship. It's only six months. You sure you're going to be okay here without me?"

Sean shrugged. "We talked about this. We have everything in place as much as we could. You have all the recipes lined up for the next six months. Your assistant brewmaster knows what he's doing to hold the fort. And we can call you. It's not ideal, but we planned for this. The question is, are you sure this is the right move for you?"

I stared at him. "Of course it is. It rounds out my brewmaster education."

Sean sighed. "I don't mean that, though. Do you really need it? I mean, you did all the education and received all of your certifications here in the States. Do you need to go to Germany?"

"They make the best beer around. Think of what I could learn." Sean wasn't asking me anything I hadn't thought of before, especially since I had come home to Holly Creek and Sadie.

He made a noncommittal sound. "I understand wanting to be the best at what you do, but I actually wasn't talking about that. I mean, it's not really my business, but are you sure this is the best move, considering Sadie?"

He fell into step beside me as we walked back toward to the Biergarten and our tent. Sadie. Would she understand? When I explained I needed to do this to expand my knowledge and grow my business, of course she would, right? It was only six months. I would be back when it was over.

She would understand. Right?

CHAPTER TWENTY-SEVEN

SADIE

The rest of Oktoberfest passed in a blur of activity, tourists, laughter, and chaos. But overall, the festival was a resounding success, or so it appeared. Turnout had been much higher than it had been in previous years, owing largely to the social media blitz that had been done and the media blowout that Tap Meister had added. The town was in the mood to celebrate, along with many tourists who had stayed to enjoy the evening entertainment.

Everyone gathered that evening in the Biergarten tent for dancing and music from a German group, and there was much laughter along with a lot of joy. I sat on one of the back tables, watching my fellow townspeople talk and laugh and mingle with the out-of-towners, all having a wonderful time. This was why I loved my town, loved the small-town atmosphere. I couldn't imagine living anywhere else.

Someone slid into the seat next to me, and a beer magically appeared, along with a soft pretzel and a plastic cup of mustard. "You looked like you needed sustenance after dancing that, whatever it was."

I laughed. "It's a traditional German or Bavarian line dance called, and I'm sure I'm going to butcher the pronunciation, Anton Aus Tirol. I can't believe you don't remember it."

Jaxon grimaced. "I was always too cool to dance back then. I was too busy trying to sneak some beer."

I ripped off a piece of pretzel, dipped it in the mustard, and held it out to him. He nipped it from my fingers, sucking on them for good measure. I shivered at the sensual promise in his gaze. Since we'd starting seeing each other again, I'd been so damned insatiable, though recently, I could sense something was off with Jaxon. I'd put it down to the stress of taking over Tap Meister and getting ready for Oktoberfest, but I had a niggling feeling that it was something else.

I took a bite of pretzel for myself and sighed. It was still warm. The salt and tart mustard were a perfect complement to the dough. Yum. I opened my eyes to see his heated gaze on me. I blushed and tried to focus on anything but sex.

"So did you succeed? At sneaking beer?"

He grinned. "Well, Jed would occasionally slip me one, as long as no one else was around. But most of the time, nope. No luck."

I frowned. "Why was he so difficult about selling to you then? You would think that he would love to have you take over since you spent so much time there."

Jaxon looked away and took a deep swallow of his beer. "Do you like the new Oktoberfest brew? I thought it had a light taste but a solid hint of fall notes."

Obligingly, even though beer wasn't my thing, I took a sip. He was right. It was light, almost refreshing, with almost a maple flavor to it, but not too sweet. Even the color was a clear gold, not heavy or dark. "It's wonderful. What did you name it?"

"Harvest Hues Amber Ale. A little on the nose, since most beers have that amber and gold color that reminds me of the fall leaves, but naming things is not my forte. Glad you liked it."

I laid a hand on his arm. "Don't think I didn't notice you changing the subject. Why was Jed difficult about selling?"

He sighed and stared at the dancers in the square. "Hard to say. I'm sure he wasn't happy to give it all up. He'd run Tap Meister a long time and loved this place."

"He must have known that you loved it too. You were his shadow for so long."

He shrugged, a casual toss that belied how much I knew Jed had meant to him over the years. "He taught me a lot about making beer. After my mom died, I spent a lot of time here, coming in with my dad when he worked here. Jed never saw me as a nuisance. Lila was off with her friends, but I loved it here." He paused and sipped his beer, his expression troubled. "Dad and Jed had a falling out when I was in high school. I don't know what it was about, not exactly, but I think it was about my dad's drinking and him not being as reliable as he had been."

I stared at Jaxon, shocked by his words. I knew his father had struggled, especially after Jaxon had left for college, seemed to struggle with daily life and activities around his house. Lila and her husband did a lot for the older man, grocery shopping, yard work, checking in on him. But she never said anything about what was wrong, and I never pried. It didn't seem right. The few times I had seen him around town, he had been angry and blamed me for Jaxon leaving home. He seemed depressed and angry, but maybe something more had been going on. What kind of friend had I been not to help Lila out more?

"Jaxon, I'm so sorry. I didn't know." I laid a hand on his forearm, feeling the tense muscles under my touch.

He gave a half-smile. "He's doing much better. Honestly, Lila and I think he had issues after mom died but shoved it down. We're not sure what triggered it, but he's struggled. Lila has taken the brunt of it and Tom has been amazing. Dad is doing better, but he still resents me for leaving."

"Have you talked to him?"

He laughed, a raw, hoarse sound. "I think you were the easier one to talk to. He's been stubborn."

I chuckled. "You won me over. You can do the same with him."

He pulled me to his side and kissed me. "I don't think my amazing bedroom skills will help in this instance."

I rolled my eyes, but before I could reply, a shadow fell across our table. Nancy Sloane stood there in a pair of stylish jeans that fit her slim frame perfectly and a teal blouse that was more suited to a night out for dinner than an Oktoberfest party on the green. She had an amused expression on her face.

"May I join you for a moment?"

Jaxon tensed next to me but nodded. She slid into a seat and gave us a broad smile. "Well, I hope you don't mind a little business talk. I get most of my best business conversations at places like this."

"Doesn't leave much room for fun, does it?" Jaxon replied.

She pointedly looked around her. "And weren't you both working all day?"

He smothered a rueful grin. "Touché."

"So down to brass tacks. You asked me to find places to lease or rent, or even buy. The market is tight right now, especially around Holly Creek. But I've found you a few places to look at that I think match your requirements. I'll email you the list later, but I don't have to tell you that we need to hurry if you want to get in first on these places."

My heart leapt inside. "You never told me that you contacted Nancy! This is great news!"

Jaxon didn't appear as excited as I did. A muscle ticked in his jaw as he stared at the room. Finally, he refocused back on us. "I spoke with her a couple of weeks ago. Anything I should be alerted to now? Highlights?"

He sounded so distant, formal. It was weird. But Nancy didn't seem to think anything of it. She pulled out her phone and tapped a few things in. "I put an outlier on the list. The Holden house. You're from the area, so you're probably familiar with it. It's an older home, Federal Village style, but they have updated it quite a bit. The Holdens want to winter somewhere warmer, test living in Myrtle Beach. They may consider selling or they might not. So for now, the house is a short-term rental. Whoever rents has first shot at purchasing."

"But they could also be pushed out at the end of winter."

Nancy nodded. "They committed to staying until April, seven months from now. It's ready to move in now. But you could be in the same boat in April. Or you could be first in line to buy it before it even goes on the market. And you know it will go fast."

I held my breath. The Holden house had been my favorite home for years. I knew they had been thinking of moving south for a few years, ever since Ella Holden had broken her leg on the ice on her front steps. But Arnie Holden resisted, not wanting to live in the heat and humidity. It sounded like they had found a balance they could agree on. I wished I was in a position to rent the house or bid on it to buy it. But I couldn't risk my place right now on a temporary rental, and I couldn't buy, not as I was still getting the shop up and running.

Jaxon could, but did he want a temporary rental?

I turned to him to gauge his reaction, but his expression was still closed off, shut down. He nodded at Nancy. "Thank you. I might not want to risk being kicked out just after settling in. Let me review the list and I'll call you Monday, okay?"

She didn't appear to see anything strange in his reaction. She gave a brisk nod and stood. "By the way, great job on the beer. I'm not much of a beer girl. I prefer vodka martinis, but it's all that was served. And I approve. Welcome home."

I waited until she had moved on before I turned to him. "The Holden house? That would be amazing, right?"

He shrugged, his expression still tight and closed off. "But it's a big risk. Seven months and then I could be right back where I am now."

"Or you could be in the position to make an offer."

He wasn't acting like himself. I was used to the Jaxon who went after what he wanted, who was positive and determined. This Jaxon was already expecting it to fail, to be a disaster. If that Jaxon had been in control before he bought the brewery, we would never have gotten back together. So why now? Why be so confident it would fail?

"Do you know something the rest of us don't? Like maybe the Holdens won't like South Carolina?"

He turned his attention fully to me. "I don't have any inside knowledge, if that's what you're implying. I just don't want to be waiting for the axe to fall, for them to change their minds."

I hesitated because my first thought had been maybe he could move in with me if that happened, but I wasn't sure where we'd be in our relationship then. Hell, I wasn't sure where we were right now. I couldn't shake the feeling that, while we spent every night together and shared our bodies, there was something off between us. We weren't quite aligned, and after the disaster ten years ago, I needed to be absolutely sure that we were solid before making any commitments beyond what we already had.

I stood and tugged him to his feet. "Well, keep an open mind and check out the other places on her list. Maybe something will be right for you. Now this is a festival, a celebration. Let's dance!"

He followed me onto the dance floor, and we had fun the rest of the night. But it still felt like a part of him wasn't there with me.

CHAPTER TWENTY-EIGHT

JAXON

Sunday evening, I spoke with the brewery coordinators who managed the internship where I was going to be studying in Germany, ironing out the details about when I had to arrive, travel arrangements, living details, and the duration. I didn't spend that night with Sadie, not knowing how to break the news to her. It was cowardly, but I needed time to find a way to tell her about this.

I filled my night with Tap Meister details. Sean and I worked out brewery coverage. Fortunately, Doug Edwards, the previous brewmaster at Tap Meister, had wanted to stay on for continuity and would help us while I was gone. I had a week to transition the new brew recipes to him before I had to leave. And tell Sadie, of course.

I should have gone to see her Monday, so of course, I procrastinated and went to my father's house to help rake up the leaves that had fallen and piled up in his backyard. I had been raking for a solid hour before Dad emerged from the sliding back door and came out on the deck to watch me. I braced myself for his criticism, because of course I never did anything right. Never raked right. Never shoveled right. Never mowed right. As if it mattered how you did it. The point was the leaves removed, the snow gone, and the grass cut, right? But not to my father.

When he only stood there staring at me, my shoulders slowly relaxed, and I kept going, raking the leaves into a center pile. I hadn't realized how overgrown the backyard had gotten in the decade since I'd been gone. The trees that had provided gentle shade now hung over the house, towering and looming, keeping the backyard in perpetual gloom and more leaves on the ground than I ever remembered. The grass struggled to grow without much sunlight, leaving patches of dirt and exposed roots of the older trees. The playscape area was nicely kept up, thanks to Tom and Lila, but with the storms we got in northwestern New York State, I worried that these trees, or even a large limb, could damage the house. Yet another thing to worry about when I would be half a world away, though I knew Tom and Lila could manage it. They had been doing just fine without me for the past several years.

I straightened and arched my back, feeling a few pops in my spine. My dad stood there, on the other side of the pile of leaves, holding a glass of iced tea. "You should stay hydrated. Your mother used to yell at me about that all the time."

I arched my eyebrow at the drink of choice but took the glass gratefully. I was thirsty and drank half of it in a single go.

"Beer isn't good for when you're working outside, or so your sister's husband tells me."

"He's a doctor, so I suppose he would know," I replied noncommittally.

Dad shrugged. "I guess. Your mother hated when I would have a beer while working in the yard. She'd worry that I would get hurt or something."

It had been a long time since I'd thought about my mom.

She'd passed away when I was in junior high, and I'd stuffed it all down deep inside because Dad never wanted to speak about her. Lila and I would talk between ourselves, but even we stopped after a while. Our family unraveled after she passed, though we put Band-Aids over the wound to keep going for a while.

"I don't remember her that well," I admitted.

Dad looked sad for a moment, his shoulders sagging, and I realized that he'd gotten old. His hair had thinned and gone gray. His face was lined with age and disappointment. His clothes were simple and probably the same that he'd had when I was in high school—a pair of jeans that were worn in several spots, a thin blue striped shirt that had seen better years and was probably in fashion before the turn of the twenty-first century, and sneakers that needed replacing. I knew Lila tried to help him, but Dad was stubborn, or maybe he didn't care anymore.

"She would have been proud of you."

His words hit me in the heart, and I sucked in a breath to cover the pain. "Would she? Are you?"

He looked startled. "Of course she would. You got a college education. You own your own business. The only thing she would have liked to see is you married with a couple of kids. But you're still young yet."

I leaned on the rake. "That's great, Dad. I'm glad Mom would have been happy. What about you? I know I disappointed you, and I'm sorry."

He jerked up straighter, then settled back into the slightly hunched position. "What do you mean, disappointed me? I'm not disappointed. I missed you while you were gone, but I'm proud of you."

His words completely rocked my world, and I tried to reconcile that with the man who sat me down after every football game and made me go over every mistake to ensure I was better next time so I could get that scholarship, go further, maybe go professional. Where was that man?

"I never played football like you wanted. Not even at college, despite my scholarship." I was a little bitter over that but, honestly, I was okay with the decision. It was never my long-term goal.

He limped around the giant pile of leaves that Tom and Lila's kids would love to jump in and laid a surprisingly heavy hand on my shoulder. "Son, you got hurt. That happens sometimes. I'm just glad you came through it okay. You got lucky. I have this bum knee from my playing days. Hurts like a bitch, especially when the weather acts up. And it always acts up in New York. I just never wanted you to have regrets. I wanted to make sure you always went for what you really wanted and never let anyone hold you back. If you're happy, then that's all that matters. Are you happy?"

Well, shit. Where did this all come from?

"I'm going to Germany, Dad. I got an internship to study under some brewmasters over there. It will really help me elevate my knowledge and experience so I can expand and grow Tap Meister. I leave in a week."

He blinked at me, as if surprised by my change in topic. "Well. That's a surprise. I thought you had moved back to Holly Creek for good. Didn't expect you to be leaving so soon. What does your business partner think?"

Sean had been supportive, thank goodness. He understood why I felt I needed to do it. "He supports this. Douglas Edwards is staying on to take my spot until I come back. I've started the winter brew, so Douglas only has to keep it going and the other beers we already have in process. Those he already knows better than I do."

Dad nodded, staring at the pile of assorted colored dead

leaves. "What about Sadie? She okay with you going half a world away? How long you going for?"

I sighed. "I haven't told her yet. Still looking for the right words."

Dad narrowed his gaze at me and studied me for a long moment. "Son, I know I wasn't the best father all the time. We had our ups and downs. But are you sure you're doing the right thing, leaving now when you just got back? You hurt that girl real bad when you left the first time. She may not forgive you again."

"I'm not leaving. I'm just taking a short-term business opportunity. It's just six months. Then I'll be back, and everything will be fine." Why did everyone ask me that?

He eyed me skeptically. "Well, I don't know much about women. But I don't think she'll take it very easily. I hope Germany is worth it."

Sadie would understand. Just like I would understand if she got an amazing opportunity in France or Switzerland. But a tiny voice inside said, *If you're so confident that she'll understand, why haven't you told her yet?*

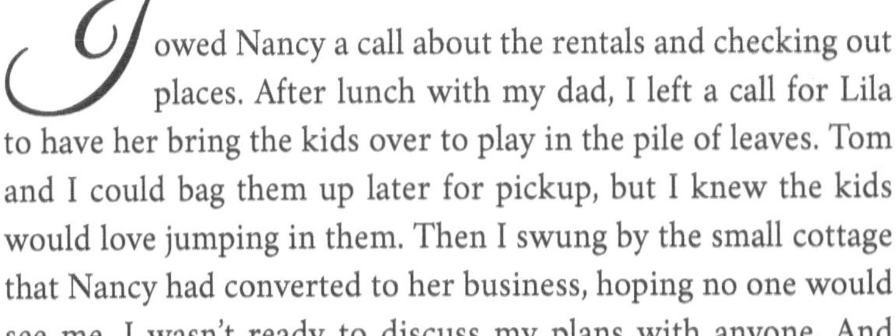

owed Nancy a call about the rentals and checking out places. After lunch with my dad, I left a call for Lila to have her bring the kids over to play in the pile of leaves. Tom and I could bag them up later for pickup, but I knew the kids would love jumping in them. Then I swung by the small cottage that Nancy had converted to her business, hoping no one would see me. I wasn't ready to discuss my plans with anyone. And Sadie needed to hear it from me. If I ever got the balls to do it.

Fortunately, Nancy's office was free of customers, so she ushered me in after offering me a coffee first. I declined, and we got down to business. Without getting into detail, I that explained I needed to delay any rental for six months.

Nancy blinked for a moment. "I thought you were looking for something immediately. Did I misunderstand?"

"No, something came up, and I might not be in the area for a few months, so a rental would stand empty."

She nodded slowly. "So the Holden house would be out, unfortunately. I had mentioned your name, and they were very excited, hoping you would be interested. I believe you know them?"

I nodded. "Mrs. Holden taught seventh grade English, and her husband coached the junior varsity team. So yeah, I know them well. But I can't rent their place knowing I won't be here. And when I come back, I might only have a month or so before they come home."

"They might not come home at all," she gently reminded me.

"You're pushing the house pretty hard, Nancy. What aren't you telling me?"

She grimaced. "Fine. The Holdens are particular about who they rent to. They want to be sure the place won't be damaged, especially if they decide to come home. If they decide to sell, well, that's a different situation. But they're leaving their furniture and belongings for the renter. They want to know it will be taken care of."

I knew Sadie would have loved that house. She'd said as much on Saturday, and growing up, she'd always loved that old home.

I stood. "I'm sorry, Nancy. If it goes on the market or up for rent in the spring, I'm interested. But I am delaying my rental search until March. Can you prepare some options for me for then?"

We ran through my requirements and the updated timeline. When we were done, we stood, and she shook my hand. "I wish you all the best in Germany. I'll keep it quiet, as you requested.

If I hear any updates on the Holden house, I'll keep you posted. And I'll send you some rentals or buy options in February."

"Thanks, Nancy. Appreciate your flexibility."

I left feeling like I was leaving a great opportunity on the table. But I was doing the right thing. Now to tell Sadie. Maybe tonight over dinner.

CHAPTER TWENTY-NINE

SADIE

I was restocking the display cases after the Oktoberfest weekend. The tourists had flooded our small town and had bought a lot of chocolate to take home. It was wonderful. As a businesswoman, I was thrilled. As a creative, I had to get my butt in the kitchen and start making more, especially since this was the height of leaf peeping season and more tourists would be here by the weekend. It was a lot of work, but I was thrilled to do it. More chocolate meant more sales, and more sales meant potential expansion, and I was all about that.

In addition, I could start planning for the holiday season and Christmas, the most wonderful time of year. Holly Creek went all out for Christmas, hosting several events throughout the season including sleigh rides, Santa events, tree decorating and more. I couldn't wait for the season and needed to start preparing the store. And I had the wedding to think of. Chelsea's wedding was a couple of days before Christmas in the city. I was providing the favors and I had my bridesmaid's duties to perform. There was a lot to juggle. At least I had found my date for the wedding and covered that stupid bet early. Now I wouldn't have to worry about that!

Clara had run to get us some lunch, so I was manning the front of the store, not that I expected a lot of business. But I didn't want to be elbow deep in chocolate and have to leave it. That could ruin the chocolate or make a customer wait. Neither was a good option. Besides, I could use the break to assess the stock we had and reset the displays. It was too early to add some Christmas cheer. Customers got a little touchy if you put out Christmas too early when they were still enjoying the fall season, but I slipped in a few evergreen and holly branches here and there. A subtle homage to the town's name.

The bells above the door jingled merrily, and I looked up to see Douglas Edwards walk in, a sheepish look on his face. I grinned because I knew exactly why he was looking so abashed.

"Good afternoon, Douglas. How can I help you today?"

He shuffled to the counter, still not meeting my gaze. "You'd think I'd remember after all these years. We got married Oktoberfest weekend thirty-nine years ago. And yet somehow I still managed to forget. Abigail Hubbard is putting together a bouquet for Annette, and now I need some special chocolates to sweeten her toward me."

I stifled my grin. "Every year, Douglas. At least as long as I've been here. Maybe you need to go for something bigger. Like a cruise."

Annette had made no secret of her desire to go on one of those Alaskan cruises to see the glaciers and the whales. She was not a fan of the Caribbean. Said she would burn in that tropical sun and Douglas would be bored to tears. But Alaska. That would be an adventure. How he missed her blatant hints was beyond me. But then again, he had forgotten their anniversary every year, and it fell around Oktoberfest, so who was I to judge?

He winked at me. "Oh, never fear. I'm not that thick in the

head, though Annette might disagree. I know she wants a cruise. I've already been down to the travel office to book one for next year. It's too late for this year and besides, I'm needed at the brewery."

He began perusing the chocolates, and I grabbed a box for his selection. "I thought you would have retired with the new ownership. Isn't Jaxon taking your spot as brewmaster?"

He grinned. "Yes, and he's very smart, too. Has some new ideas that I think will be good for Tap Meister. His fall beer was excellent and already receiving great reviews from shops and restaurants in the region. No, I agreed to stay on to help with the original recipes and then take over while he's gone."

He pointed out a few chocolates, not realizing that I had frozen in place, his words like a bucket of ice water on a cold winter's day. "Douglas, what do you mean, while he's gone? Who's gone?"

He glanced up at me. "Well, Jaxon, of course. He'll be in Germany for a while. Several months, at least. He'll set up our winter beers, which are already started, and I'll work on them while he's gone."

I swallowed past a thick throat. "When was this discussed?"

"Oh, I think it happened in the past few days. When they took over, it was mentioned as a possibility, but it was only confirmed today."

I nodded and pasted a fake smile on my face when Douglas gave me an odd look. "I see. Sorry, which chocolates did you want?"

I swiftly packaged the gift, adding a few flourishes to make it special, then rang him up, giving him a generous discount for his anniversary. He left with a big smile, and I sank to my stool, my hands shaking and my entire world narrowing to a spot right in front of my eyes.

Jaxon had known since he'd come back that he was leaving. He had planned to leave all along, after promising me that he was staying. He had lied to me. No wonder he didn't want his own place and avoided any conversations about looking at places with Nancy. He didn't plan to be here. How could he buy a business and then be so irresponsible to leave right after taking over?

My blood pounded in my ears, and I swayed on the stool, caught in a maelstrom of emotion. Anger, heartbreak, rage, despair, fury, grief. I didn't even know what to say or do. I just sat there, my emotions a chaotic mess inside.

A hand landed gently on my shoulder. "Sadie? Are you okay? I've been calling your name for like five minutes now."

I turned to Clara and could barely make her out through the glaze of tears in my eyes.

"Oh my God, Sadie. What happened?" Clara gasped and pulled me into the back room so we'd be out of the view of any customers who came in.

I was numb but followed her blindly. She set me down on a chair and pulled another one up in front of me. She clasped both of my hands and leaned into me. "Sadie, what happened?"

I shook my head. "Jaxon's leaving."

She sagged back against the chair. "What do you mean, leaving? Did he stop by? Where is he going? I don't understand."

I quickly told her what Douglas had said, and she snarled. "I can't believe he would do that to you or to Tap Meister. He just took over. How could he just leave?"

I shook my head, feeling so tired suddenly. "I don't know, Clara. But the real question is, why didn't he tell me?"

She snorted. "Obviously, he knew you would be pissed. And rightly so."

"Was he just going to leave? Or tell me at the last minute? He's known this was a possibility for a couple of months. He told me he was here to stay. He lied. Why would he do that?"

Clara gripped my hand again. "I don't know, honey. You need to ask him that."

My phone dinged with a text, and I picked it up. I grunted. "Looks like I'll get my chance. He's invited me for dinner. Tonight."

"What are you going to say?"

That was a good question. I only wished I had an answer.

Despite Clara's insistence on me taking the rest of the day off, I worked. It was better for me to lose myself in making chocolate rather than stew at home about Jaxon and his plans. Not that I didn't dwell on those thoughts while working, but at least I didn't wallow, as much as I would have if I was alone.

I wanted to call Lila, to see if she knew about his plans. Part of me didn't want to know. I hoped she didn't know about this, hadn't kept it from me like she'd kept him living a few hours away or moving back. I didn't want to put her in the middle. I understood her divided loyalties honestly. He was her brother, the one who had been there for her after her mom died. But damn it, if she knew about this and didn't tell me, our friendship might have a ways to go in recovering.

I went home and showered to clean off the chocolate smell and help with my puffy eyes. Then I carefully dressed in a nice pair of black leggings and a teal tunic cabled sweater. I hadn't been to Jaxon and Sean's place, so this was a new adventure. I was glad we were meeting there. It would make it easier for me to leave when I was ready and not have to ask Jaxon to go. I was afraid he might fight me and I would be too weak to say no. Damn it, I still loved him, even if he broke my heart. This time, I feared the fractures were too much to overcome. I wasn't sure I could forgive this.

I drove through the streets of Holly Creek, trying to figure out what I was going to say and what I wanted. Did I want him to stay when he clearly didn't want to? No, even I couldn't ask that of him. Throughout the afternoon of thinking through this whole situation, I guess I had gone through the stages of anger and grief, and now I just wanted answers. I was resigned to the situation, resigned to knowing that I wasn't important enough for him to tell me about his plans, his life. Just like ten years ago when he had ideas and dreams but didn't want to or couldn't tell me about them. A relationship can't be built on that. No one that I wanted to be a part of.

So apparently, my decision was made. Now all I needed were the explanations. Then I could move on to the alcohol and girl-friend gatherings.

I parked in the driveway and saw the lights on in the windows and took a bracing breath. I walked up the walkway and knocked on the door.

Jaxon called from inside, "It's open."

I walked in and followed the sounds down the hallway to the kitchen where he was bouncing between pans on the stove. He stopped and gave me a brilliant smile and made as if to kiss me.

I took a step back. "Do you have some news to share?"

His face fell as understanding hit him.

CHAPTER THIRTY

JAXON

My chest tightened at Sadie's calm, almost dispassionate tone. She knew. Somehow, she had found out about me leaving and had waited until tonight to confront me. And judging by her eerily blank expression and distance, she had already worked through the worst of the emotional reactions, which didn't bode well for me. For us.

Fuck. How could I salvage this? I set the steaks aside since they were done and covered them with a lid to keep them warm. I wiped my hands on my apron and grabbed two wine glasses.

"Why don't we talk about this at the table?"

"I don't need the wine. Just tell me the truth. Are you leaving?"

I took a deep breath past the band that wrapped around my chest. "Yes. I'm going to Germany for an internship to study beer-making with a famous brewmaster. It's a hard program to get into, and I wasn't sure I would even be accepted."

She folded her arms in front of her, still not budging from the doorway, her body stiff and uncompromising. "When did you know about this?"

"Friday." I didn't lie. I needed to tell the whole truth, even if it damned me in her eyes.

Judging by the way her eyes widened and betrayal flooded them, she had suspected that but hoped she was wrong. "So you lied to me. All weekend, you knew you were leaving and couldn't be bothered to tell me about it."

I set the bottle and glasses down carefully and took the few steps across the small kitchen to her, taking her shoulders gently in my hands. "Sadie, I wanted to tell you, but I needed more information. All they told me was that I had been accepted. I had to have a call with them on Sunday to find out more information, when I was going, how long, that kind of thing."

"When did you apply?"

I glanced away from her accusing glare. That was a trickier topic. "I applied in the spring."

She wrenched out of my grasp and stalked past me into the attached eating area. "So you knew you might leave when you came back, yet you still told me that you were here to stay? That you weren't going to leave again?"

"Damn it, Sadie. I'm not leaving. I'm just taking an opportunity for a short time. It's six months. I'll be back when it's over."

She hugged herself tightly. "I've heard that before. *I'm only going to college. I'll be home after. I'm just taking this opportunity, then I'll be back. I think we should see other people to be sure.* You say a lot of things, Jaxon. And then you do something else. And I get left behind. Every single fucking time while I wait for you like a chump. Not this time. I can't do it again. Fool me once, shame on me. Fool me twice, fuck you."

She pushed past me to leave, but I blocked her, not willing to let her go, not yet. "Goddamn it, Sadie. I thought we got past all that."

She stared up at me, tears in her eyes. "So did I. But clearly, I was the fool."

"I'm coming back. I have a business here. I'm not going to run out on that. Sean manages the business side and I run the beer. I have to be the best at making the beer. I have to be at the top of my game or we don't have a brewery. It all rests on my shoulders. This internship gives me that leg up on the competition."

She pulled back. "And what about the next great opportunity? The next big thing? Will you leave then? Are we just a port in the storm until you find something better? Or someone?"

I reared back at the venom in her tone. "Sadie, there's never been anyone else like you. You've always been the one for me. Always. If you doubt that, then maybe we should take a break."

She gave a raw, harsh laugh that had nothing to do with humor. "A break, yeah right. No, not a temporary break, but a permanent one. We're done, Jaxon. I can't do this again. I won't do this again. Goodbye."

And she swept past me and out of my life, leaving me stunned and broken.

S ean found me sitting at the kitchen table a few hours later, the bottle of wine empty, along with a six-pack of our beer. Probably a waste of excellent beer since I'd barely tasted it. My primary goal was to get drunk off my ass and forgot what Sadie had said to me. I didn't even bother with dinner, leaving it on the stove, though I had remembered to turn off the burners. Another waste of good filet mignon. Sean could enjoy it when he came home, if it wasn't spoiled.

He grabbed a beer from the fridge and came over to the table. The chair gave an audible screech against the old linoleum floor, and I winced. He murmured an apology and sat, leveling a hard stare at me. "I take it the talk didn't go well?"

"She already knew."

He nodded. "I saw Douglas tonight. He mentioned he'd stopped in to her shop for chocolates for his anniversary and may have shared news that he thought was common knowledge. For what it's worth, he apologizes."

I shrugged, still staring at the remaining beer in the bottle. "It was for the best. I could only imagine how much more pissed she would have been if I had sprung it on her cold."

He sighed. "What happened?"

"She accused me of always leaving, looking for something better while using Holly Creek and her as a for-now kind of thing. I'm paraphrasing, by the way."

"I assumed." He took a swallow of his beer. "Is it true?"

"Hell no, it's not true." I exploded out of my seat and paced the small kitchen eating area. "How could you even think that?"

Sean only watched me with that impassive, calm gaze of his. "Well, you couldn't wait to get out of this town. Avoided coming home as much as you could. As soon as you came back, you're leaving, even though you bought a business here. And you don't even have a place to live that's yours. Man, I have to say, it doesn't look good for you."

I stopped and glared at him. "Whose side are you on?"

"Who says I have to be on someone's side, Jax? I'm giving you the perspective that Sadie has. And asking you, are you sure you want to be here? Because it doesn't seem like you do."

I growled in my throat, anger rising like bile. "Do you want out of the business? Is that it?"

Sean got to his feet. "Give me a break. That's bullshit and you know it. I gave up my entire career to go in on this with you. I'm all in. But, like Sadie, I deserve to know if you're in, too." He softened his voice. "I understand why you want to do this internship. I do. The timing could be better, to be honest, for us and for you and Sadie. You just got back with her, and it's possible she'll feel like you're deserting her...again."

My throat felt tight, constricted. I couldn't lose my best friend too. "Do you feel the same way? That I'm deserting you?"

He shook his head. "Nah, man. I said I understand, and I do. It's not ideal timing, but we're also not up and rolling at full steam yet. There's still a lot to do with distribution, retail connections to continue to nurture. That's my part, and if I hire an assistant like we've been talking about, it'll help me keep up. If you think this internship will elevate our beer to the next level, then do it. We need the product to stand out. That makes for an easier sell. But if you're doing this to prove something to someone, you're already fucking awesome."

His words swamped me with relief. I wasn't losing Sean. He had as much to lose from the business as I did. We both sunk everything into Tap Meister. He had a well-paying, prestigious job before surprising me and walking away from it to become my partner. Honestly, he was the only reason I could take this internship. If I hadn't had a partner, I couldn't go. And his business knowledge, along with his negotiating the deal, was critical. I owed him everything.

I gripped his shoulder, staring into his eyes, willing him to believe what I was about to say. "Thank you, man. I owe you for everything. You're the best partner and friend I could have. I could never do this without you."

Sean grimaced. "Beer and wine, dude? Man, you are going to be so sick tomorrow."

I reared back. "I'm trying to be meaningful here."

He snorted. "You're being a sappy drunk. I haven't heard you like this since college. Let's fast forward. Yeah, you owe me for holding down the fort and keeping your ass afloat. Got it. Now, let's get you a nice big glass of water, two aspirin, then pour you into bed. Then you can figure out your mess with Sadie."

He gently shoved me into a chair and went to the sink for supplies. I shook my head. "I think it's over for real this time. She said we were done. Over. I think if I go, I'll lose her forever."

He handed me two pills and the glass, which I took. "Then you have a choice to make, don't you? Stay and keep Sadie…or go and possibly lose her."

I finished the glass. "Why can't she understand that this is my job? This is a great opportunity for me to learn and expand the business? It could be good for Holly Creek, too. She would love that. She loves this town. Oh, I should have told her that. Maybe she would have understood."

I fumbled for my phone, and Sean neatly lifted it from my hands. "Nope, no phone until you're sober. Trust me, you don't want to be flooding her phone with drunken messages. Call her in the morning with sober, coherent thoughts."

He tucked the phone in his back pocket and lifted me from the chair. "Now, off to bed."

I followed him, leaning a little more than usual. But I had a plan. She had to see that I was doing this for the right reasons, right? I could win her back. I had to.

CHAPTER THIRTY-ONE

SADIE

I couldn't believe I'd fallen for him again. I hadn't learned the first time. I had to go back for more. I whipped the chocolate furiously. Who needed a mixer when I had fury feeding me today? I buried myself in my work, staying in the back while Clara worked the front and eyed me with concern, though she never said a word.

"Here you are. I've been calling you all morning, worried sick about you." Lila stood in the back doorway, her face pulled tight with worry.

I barely spared her a glance. "I turned off my phone."

I didn't want to tell her that I was avoiding her brother, though I suspected she already knew. I'd woken up to dozens of text messages and calls from him. Though, surprisingly, only a couple from last night. I wasn't sure if that was a good sign or not. But I wasn't calling him back or even listening to find out. I blocked his number and muted his texts, but not confident that he wouldn't find a way around that, I'd finally turned it off completely.

"So he sent you."

Lila frowned. "No, he didn't send me. I can't believe you would think that. I'm your friend."

I gave her a look. "You kept other things from me. Did you know about this?"

That had bothered me all day yesterday and last night. I had sworn I wouldn't ask her about it, wouldn't say anything because it didn't matter, but, in the end, it did matter. Lila was my friend, and I needed to know if she knew Jaxon had planned to leave when she'd persuaded me to give him another chance.

She braced herself on the other side of the worktable across from me and stared right into my eyes. "I didn't know he had an internship in Germany or had applied for one. I would have ripped him a new one, trust me. Nor would I have pushed you back together with him. Honestly, I would have advised you to wait until he came back."

"Assuming he comes back," I muttered.

She cocked her head. "Of course he's coming back. He has a business here."

I set the bowl and whisk down. "Lila, plenty of people have businesses run by other people. He doesn't have to live here to own a business here. And even if he comes back, what's keeping him from running off again? I don't know what he's running from, but until he figures it out, I'm done. Maybe even then, I'm done."

She sighed and pulled a stool over. "I don't understand it. I wish I did. And I'm so sorry. I had really hoped this was going to work out for you both. You'd get your date to the wedding and your own happily ever after."

I snorted. "I'm beginning to think that I'm not meant for a happily ever after."

"He's one guy. It might be different with someone else."

I sagged onto a stool. "The matchmaker said he was my soul mate. I didn't really believe it, not at the time, and I didn't want to accept it was him, but, Lila, I started to believe it."

I fumbled for my phone and turned it on, waiting for the system to come back online and all the notifications from unknown numbers to ding. I navigated to my email. "See this? I met this woman at the festival. Her name is Theresa. Her sister convinced her to give it a shot, and she met someone. The matchmaker said he was her one. They're getting married in the spring. In Lovelorn."

Lila's eyes widened. "Damn, that was quick."

"I know. Part of me wants to say it was too quick, but I saw them together, and they really were too cute." I dropped the phone on the table. "I'm happy for her, really happy. But why can't I find that?"

Lila reached across the table and gripped my hand. "Maybe it's not you, Sadie. Maybe this time it really is him."

I snorted. "I've heard that before. But maybe it's both of us. I'm not enough to keep him, and he is still searching for whatever he needs. Either way, I need to move on."

Lila nodded sadly. "I'm sorry, honey. I feel terrible for pushing you back together. He's my brother, and I could kick his ass for you, if that helps."

I burst out laughing, thinking of a petite Lila kicking Jaxon's ass. "I'd pay money to see that, but not necessary. I've learned my lesson. Cher was right. You can't turn back time."

She frowned. "Really not sure what Cher has to do with this, but okay. Girls' night to drown your sorrows?"

"Maybe this weekend. I'm just not ready."

I knew Lila just wanted to help, was desperate to assuage what she felt was guilt over her role in this breakup, but it wasn't her fault. I wasn't quite up to a girls' night yet, not even where I could bash Jaxon. Right now, I wanted to lick my wounds in peace and get over this all. Maybe when I was past the sadness phase and into the anger, I'd be ready for that.

I stood. "I'll be fine. I survived before, and I can do it again. But damn it. I still need a date for that damned wedding!"

Lila choked, and we both laughed. It was a start.

❄

I spent the week isolated and alone, working through my issues. I wasn't ready to man-bash or bitch or complain or anything, really. I needed to figure out how I had fallen into the same trap ten years later. I needed time alone to work through everything. When I felt a little less raw and more functional, I was ready to let my friends in. It coincided with a Friday night, so that was a bonus.

Girls' night ended up in the last place I wanted to be: Courtney's place. We rotated girls' nights, and the roll of the dice fell badly for me. I almost cried off, but I knew someone, or all of them, would just drag me there. It was pure bad luck, the only kind I seemed to have lately, that it was here. The studio where I'd said I love you to Jaxon. Well, the second first time, since the first time was in high school. Neither time had really ended well. Maybe love wasn't in the cards for me.

"Don't say that," Clara slurred as she waved her glass of wine or whatever she was drinking.

There was an assortment of beverages, and no one needed to watch their drinking, since most of us stayed over where we were. Clara's poison started with wine, then on to the harder stuff. Mine usually remained with wine, though I occasionally joined in on the more festive seasonal drinks. Tonight's special was hard cider or mulled wine, for the less adventurous, or Fireball sangria for the rest of us. We liked drinks we could make in batches and not have to remake over and over. This one was a winner, and I was on my second and feeling the effects.

"I'm serious. I thought I found true love. He left me. I go to a matchmaker who supposedly finds your soul mate, and he points me right back to the same guy and what happens? He leaves me again! Something's seriously fucked up there."

"Maybe the matchmaker was wrong," Sam said. "It can happen. They only put together possibilities. You still need to make it work."

I glared at her through slightly fuzzy eyes. "Are you saying I didn't put in the work?"

Everyone hurried to assure me that wasn't what she'd meant. Sam shrugged as she finished her drink. "I'm just saying. Love is a lot like hair color. Timing is everything. You fuck that up and you have a disaster on your hands."

Courtney snorted a laugh. "I have literally never heard that. You just made it up."

Sam grinned. "Doesn't mean it isn't true. You could be meant to be together, but it's still not the right time. Or maybe the universe is wrong. Shit happens."

Shit happens was right. I was so fucking tired of it, though. "Okay, new rule. Changing the subject now. No more talk of my shitty love life and Jaxon Bigsly. Got it?"

Clara raised her hand. "We have one more order of business on that topic, sort of secondary, but related. Who are you going to the wedding with? You still need a date."

I glowered at her. "I still have a couple of months and, if all else fails, I can hire an escort."

Laughter burst out of everyone in the room, but only Courtney said what they were all thinking. "That won't work, and you know it. You can't keep a straight face when you're lying, so when someone asks you about your date, you'll spill. Then the bridesmaids will lose the bet."

"Right about now, I don't give a crap about the bet or anything, though I'm not looking forward to that embarrassing dance at the wedding if we lose. Trying to find a date got me into this mess in the first place but I'll worry about it next week. What about you? Have you found a date yet, Courtney?"

Courtney shrugged but didn't make eye contact. "I'm working on it."

Lila's gaze bounced between all of us, then she flung herself back on the bed that I refused to even sit on. "New topic. Courtney, is it okay that we're laying on your workspace? It's insanely comfortable."

Courtney shot me a quick look, then smiled. "It's fine. Not all of my photo shoots are indoors. That's why I bought this place. There are amazing locations outside too, along the river, in the woods, on the patio with the Edison lights I've strung around. So many options."

Lila made a little happy moaning noise in the back of her throat. "I can't wait to do my own shoot." She raised up to her elbows and scowled at Courtney. "Why haven't you called to set mine up yet? I told your mother at the festival that I want to do one as soon as possible." She flopped back to the bed and moved her arms languidly up and down, as if making a snow angle in the bedcovering. "I'll be alone in my photo shoot, but even then, I can't imagine being dressed so sexy outside. Or...maybe I can imagine it. Tom would love seeing me like that. In the dark, half naked, the twinkle lights glowing on my skin."

Lila continued chattering about her vision for her own shoot, and the memories of my time here welled up inside me, swamping me like a tsunami. Jaxon's body moving over mine. The feel of his hands stroking over my body. His lips feathering over my skin. The way he said I love you and me saying it back.

I stumbled to my feet, my gaze darting around the room. "I, uh, need to use the bathroom. I'll be right back."

As I raced out of the room, I heard Courtney say to Lila, "Couldn't you be a little more sensitive? Clearly, she's still raw. Her shoot was only a couple of weeks ago."

The rest of the conversation faded as I closed the door to Courtney's studio bathroom. As I splashed water on my face, a knock sounded, and I opened the door to let Courtney in. I pasted on a smile. "Sorry for being stupid."

She leaned against the counter. "You're not being stupid. You just got your heart broken. You need time. We probably should have moved our night to a different location this month."

I shook my head. "No, I'm fine. But I don't think I'll stay. I just can't."

"I understand."

Courtney reached over and wrapped a supportive arm around me, and I clutched the counter so tightly my fingers hurt. I couldn't stop thinking about that night. About what I was supposed to mean to Jaxon.

Tears leaked from beneath my lashes. "I never want to see those photos," I grumbled.

"I understand that, too."

"Have you looked at them yet?"

I jerked my head up, catching her gaze in the mirror, and silently pleaded for her to tell me that she hadn't. I didn't want to think of anyone looking at them. I didn't want to think of those photos even existing.

She silently shook her head, and I nodded. I swiped at the damned tears still slipping over my cheeks. "Delete them. Destroy them. Whatever it is you do. Those photos never see the light of day, got it?"

Courtney grimaced. "How about I hang on to them? In case you change your mind?"

I whirled around and faced her. "I won't change my mind. I never want to lay my eyes on any of them. From either of the photo shoots."

She nodded then and pulled me in for a tight hug. "Then you won't see them, sweetie. You've got my word. I'll call you a ride home, okay? You don't need to drive in this condition."

CHAPTER THIRTY-TWO

JAXON

*P*ounding at my door broke up my packing. I wasn't moving away permanently and Sean had said I could leave my stuff here instead of getting a storage unit, so that was helpful. Though I had a unit for my furniture and stuff from my last apartment, which I could have used if necessary. I only needed to pack my clothes and necessities for the six-month trip to Germany. I was only taking one suitcase and a carry-on, so not that complicated to pack, but I had dragged my feet all week in doing it. Probably because I wasn't ready to go.

I raced down the stairs, hoping it was Sadie, finally answering my messages in person. She had blocked my number, so I used Sean's and even my dad's to get through. Lila refused to help me, and Tom followed her, citing the old happy life, happy wife adage. I figured I had burned that bridge and she had chosen her side and it wasn't me. But maybe Sadie was sick of people calling her, the flower deliveries, hell, even the meal deliveries. I had tried everything to get a rise and not one response. Not even a *fuck off*.

She clearly was furious. Or she had moved on. I was hoping for the first because if she had moved on, I had no hope.

I opened the door and was immediately shoved aside by a small whirlwind. Lila berated me as soon as she walked in the door. "Seriously, Jaxon? Calls from Dad? That's a new low, even for you."

I followed her into the kitchen. "I needed her to talk to me, and she blocked my number."

"Do you blame her? You're leaving. Again."

"But I'm coming back!" I roared. "Why does everyone conveniently forget that?"

"Because maybe we're not sure you really will," Lila said quietly. She laid a hand on my arm. "Look, I know how hard it was on you growing up in Holly Creek, with Dad and everyone expecting so much from you. Everyone thought you would do all these big things. Even Dad. And I get you had to leave to figure it all out. But you've done that. When are you going to stop running?"

I dropped into the chair and ran my hands through my hair. "Lila, I'm not running. Honest. I'm just learning new techniques to help Tap Meister be better. To help me be better at brewing beer. Is that so wrong?"

She sat in the chair across from me. "Is that the only reason you're doing it? Are you sure?"

"Of course I'm sure." Wasn't I?

"I love you like a brother, which is fortunate because you are my brother, but you need some tough love right now. You've spent a long time living like a nomad, moving from job to job *learning*. And I get it. You had to do that to learn your trade. But you have your goal. What about your other goal, Sadie, marriage, a family? Or don't you want those anymore?"

I looked away because her words hit a little too close for comfort. "All my other jobs had other people to rely on for success. Tap Meister only has me. I need to be the best, so we don't screw up. This internship will ensure that I have the knowledge to make us successful. Then I can work on every-thing else."

Her eyes were sad as she looked at me. "Somehow I think you're smarter than you give yourself credit for, and I worry that you're putting too much pressure on yourself, just like back in high school." She stood and pressed a kiss to the top of my head, so much like Mom it hurt. "Don't let those pressures distract you from what's really important, Jaxon."

❄

*I*t was my last day. I had done everything I could to prepare Tap Meister for my absence. I knew they'd be fine. Sean assured me he had it all handled. He was driving me to the airport in Albany, so I didn't have to leave a car for months. He drove through the downtown of Holly Creek, right by Sadie's shop, and I slammed my hand on the dashboard.

"Stop." I needed to see her one last time, even if she kicked me out.

He gave me a doubtful glance but steered to the side of the road in front of her shop. "Are you sure this is a good idea?"

"No, but I'm doing it, anyway." I got out and headed inside, the smell of chocolate so much like Sadie.

Her assistant, Clara, looked up, her smile fading to a scowl when she saw me. She folded her arms in front of her and barri-caded the back room. "She won't see you."

"I'm headed to the airport. Let me have five minutes. She can say her piece, and I'll be gone," I pleaded, hoping she'd let me pass.

"We've said everything that needed to be said." Sadie spoke from behind me.

Hell, she hadn't even been in the shop. Clara had been faking me out, pretending Sadie was in the back room. I turned to face her, standing in the doorway, a bag of what smelled like lunch and a tray of drinks in her hand. "Five minutes is all I ask."

She walked past me toward the back room. She paused at the door. "Five minutes, then you're gone."

She walked through, and I followed, praying I had the right words. She set the bags and tray down and turned, her arms folded in front of her, her jaw set in a mulish way. "Well?"

"I fucked up. I should have been honest from the beginning. But I need to do this. It's important for the business. Can you understand that?"

She shook her head. "Of course I understand needing to do something for business. I'm a business owner too. I've had to take classes and learning experiences to improve all the time. But as I said, I also have a responsibility to the business. I can't just pick up and go willy-nilly. You're lucky that you can, especially just taking over. That's not why I'm mad."

I frowned. "But I apologized. I shouldn't have kept it from you."

"No, you shouldn't have. And you shouldn't have started a relationship saying you were staying here and never leaving. Yet you did."

"Would you have dated me otherwise?" I took a step forward, eying her warily.

"No," she said.

"So I had to do it."

"No, you had to be honest with me. How can I trust you ever again? How can I believe that you'll stay the next time? You left twice already. Come on, Jaxon. That's not a great track record."

I could feel her slipping through my fingers, though maybe she already had. I stepped back. "Okay, I see your point. When I get back in the spring, we'll talk. Maybe we can video chat and email while I'm gone."

She was already shaking her head. "You don't get it. I'm done. Don't call me. Don't email me. It's over. I'm moving on.

This time for real." She took a step forward and laid a hand on my arm. "I wish you all the best and much success. But this, between us? It's done. Goodbye, Jaxon."

My jaw clenched, and I struggled for something to say. When I came up short, I turned on my heel and strode out of the store and back to the car. Once I was buckled in, I stared straight ahead. Sean just stared at me, a question in his gaze.

"It's over. For good. Take me to the airport."

Sean let out an exhale and drove without saying a word.

CHAPTER THIRTY-THREE

SADIE

The next several weeks passed slowly, painfully. We were busy, thank God, due to the tourists come to see the changing of leaves and the fall season in our town. The shop was busy, and I focused on new recipes and testing to see what sold and what wasn't working. I decorated for the holiday, something that usually made me happy and brightened my day. But somehow, despite the bright colors and lights, it was still gray and blah. I spent more time in the kitchen area, hiring Lila to spell Clara in the front sales room on our busiest days, mostly to stop from hearing the locals ask me what had happened between Jaxon and me, when was he coming back, had I heard from him. Of course, just because I hid in my shop didn't mean they didn't accost me in the grocery story, pharmacy, or anywhere else they could. As usual, Jaxon was the primary topic, and our relationship was everyone's business, or so they thought.

I gritted my teeth through it all and said we'd decided to take a break. Unfortunately, that led to more advice that I really didn't need or want. Annette Evans told me that the secret to a happy marriage was never going to sleep angry. Of course, she also said that led to many sleepless nights while she and Douglas argued, but they always worked it out. Zeke Barrett's wife suggested that a good meal was the key to a happy marriage, though I noticed they ate out a lot. Then the icing on the cake was old Mrs. Hubbard, who discussed marital aids in the bedroom. I believe I was scarred for life after that discussion that included visual aids, instructions, and a helpful website for ordering purposes. No wonder her husband worshipped her.

Damn Jaxon for leaving me to deal with the fallout again—alone.

Of course, through all of that, pictures surfaced from the Oktoberfest. Pictures of him and me dancing, laughing, and having fun. Pictures of us at the wiener race where he awkwardly danced away from the dog peeing on his shoe while I laughed and held the trophy. Then the picture of us in the face in the hole photo booth with Jaxon as a scarecrow and me as Dorothy.

Images were posted online in social media and in the local newspaper in dribs and drabs, as if someone was purposely reminding me of how good things had been between us. When I confronted Courtney, the photographer for the event, she denied it, saying she'd handed over the photos to media coordinator for the event. It was up to them. Since I was the overall event coordinator, I should have been consulted but it seems that everyone was avoiding me, so I was left with no recourse but to grit my teeth and bare it.

My jaw hurt from the pain.

Jaxon had been gone three weeks when his business partner strolled into my store as if he didn't have a care in the world. Thanksgiving was fast approaching, as was the wedding, and I still didn't have a date. I was considering going alone and the hell with the bet. I had given Clara the day off, and Lila was preparing for her family Thanksgiving by shopping and cleaning and making everyone crazy, even though it was still a few weeks away.

I didn't really know Sean, having only met him a couple of times through Jaxon. Since then, I had avoided the brewery and anything to do with it. So I was curious why he was coming into my shop.

"Hello, Sean, right? How can I help you today?" I put on my most professional smile and waited to see what he would say.

He glanced around the shop, taking his time to peruse the offerings in each display case. "I like what you've done with your shop. It's very bright, open, welcoming. The holiday decorations are tasteful and artistic. The candy is displayed cleanly, and enticing, of course. It reminds me of a European old style candy shop."

I blushed at his words of praise, even though I knew I had nailed my shop. Jaxon had said Sean was some kind of business consultant so he analyzed businesses for success. His words of praise meant something. "Thank you. That was my goal. Are you here to analyze my business model or buy something? Or maybe something else?"

He flashed a quick grin. "I see Jaxon told you about my history as a business consultant. Sorry, I can't help but assess any small business I walk into to see how they're doing. Well done, Sadie."

I arched an eyebrow. "You'd have to look at my books to truly judge if I'm doing well or not, and that's not happening."

"Touché again. No, I'm not here to assess your business." He wandered over to the main display case where I stood and leaned on it. "I meant to come by earlier and see how you were doing. I promised Jaxon I would look in on you, but I sensed that was the last thing you'd want from me."

"Or anyone else. You guessed correctly. I can take care of

myself. Consider your duty complete." I turned away and fussed with the small Christmas tree by the register.

"But are you doing okay, Sadie? I don't know you well, and forgive me for my bluntness, but you have dark circles under your eyes. You don't look happy."

"I've also lost weight if you want to report back on that as well. It's a new diet program. It's intentional. No, Sean, you don't know me, so don't presume to know if I am happy or not."

I pushed the door to the backroom when he spoke again. "He's not happy either."

I paused, my hand on the door, my heart clenching. "I'm sorry to hear that. I don't like knowing that someone is unhappy."

"He wishes you could just talk or email or something. He misses you, Sadie. He'll be back in a few months."

I whirled around and stalked back to lean across the display. "Why does everyone focus on the fact that he'll be back soon? What about the fact that he lied, that he left? Who's saying he won't leave again? You look tired too, Sean. Putting in long hours at the brewery you just bought, trying to turn it around. Difficult to do alone, is it? He left you too."

"Yes, he did. But he left to improve our business."

I sighed, the wind taken out of my sails a bit at his words. "Well, I'm happy for you. He's helping your business but at the expense of me. Again. It's always business first, Sadie second. Maybe just once I'd like to be first. Don't I deserve that from the man who professes to love me?"

When Sean didn't reply, I straightened. "I thought so. Can I get you any chocolate? On the house since you're a friend."

"How about your sampler set? I don't think I've tried your chocolate yet."

I smiled. "I'll put together a special sampler just for you." I gathered a six-piece set and packaged it up for him. "There you go. Thanks for being a good friend to Jaxon. He needs you."

I watched him walk out of the store, only after placing a twenty on the counter, and lift his phone to his ear. The universe was testing me, but I resolved to stay strong.

CHAPTER THIRTY-FOUR

JAXON

The past month had been rough. Not exactly as I had expected from this opportunity. I was learning some great techniques I could take back with me to Tap Meister. I had even made a few changes on my weekly call with Sean and Douglas. But something was missing. Something that overshadowed the entire experience.

At first, I was angry at Sadie, angry that she couldn't understand why I had to do this. I would be back. We just needed to hold on for a few months. It wasn't a break, just a pause. But honestly, in Germany, all I had to do was work and think. I had nothing but time to do that. And I was seeing her perspective. Maybe I was wrong. The timing, everything I had promised, I had misled her. It didn't matter if it was for a week or a month or six months. I'd done exactly what I swore I would never do. I left.

Fuck. I'd really screwed up. Now how was I going to fix it from all the way in Germany when she wouldn't even read my emails, much less take a call?

My video chat rang, and I frowned. I wasn't expecting anyone to call tonight. My heart leapt. Maybe Sadie had decided to finally call me. I clicked *Accept,* and Drew Cafferty's big face filled the screen. I must have showed my disappointment because he laughed.

"Damn, sorry to disappoint you, man. I thought I'd call and congratulate you on your beers and the progress you've made with your brewery. You have done a lot in a short time. Congratulations! But clearly, that's not something you want to hear. Or maybe I'm not the someone you want to hear from?" He winked slyly at the camera.

I rolled my eyes. "Sorry, Drew. No, it's fine. I'm in Germany and was kind of hoping someone else would call."

"I'm not doing any of those weird sexting things or video porn. Sorry, man. Not my thing at all. How are you and Sadie doing? It was Sadie, right? The woman Granddad matched you with at the festival and you were headed home for?"

I let my head fall forward onto the desk with a thud, and he chuckled. "Oh, I sense trouble in paradise. Well, I am a bartender, so tell me your troubles, son."

I laughed. "You're my age, Drew." But he was a good listener, as I knew from my days in Lovelorn, so I shared everything, including my most recent revelation.

Drew nodded sagely for a few minutes after absorbing my words, then he fixed a firm gaze on me. "You fucked up. She's right. You left after promising that you'd stay. But worse than that, you chose everything else over her. Literally everything else over her. Your woman wants to be number one in your life, your priority, or at least your consideration. She didn't even get that. You, my friend, need to do some serious groveling. If she lets you."

I sighed. "That's the problem. She blocked me. Won't take my calls or emails or texts."

He stared at me. "Wow, you really are thick."

I smacked my head. "I have to do it in person."

"There it is. Finally. The lightning strikes."

"But I won't be home for five more months."

"And he misses." Drew leaned forward, his face filling the screen. "Look man, I love you. But are you really where you need to be? I was calling to tell you that your beer is outstanding. Your fall beer is one of my most popular, beating out your beer from Brimstone. Then I just got to taste your winter beer. That chocolate stout is heaven. People are going to go crazy for it. Trust me, you'll win awards for this. You know what you're doing. Are you really learning anything new there to justify your time away?"

❄

I was working through some calculations for a recipe when my email dinged. People think brewing beer is all tasting and mixing stuff, but there are a lot of calculations needed to get the perfect percentages and amounts just right for the perfect brew. Fortunately, math was always a strong subject for me.

But, there was more to owning a brewery than making beer, though you had to have the product to have a brewery. Right now, though, I felt like I was missing out on so much being half a world away. Sean had been doing a great job keeping me updated on the activities back home and every phone call we had only made me question more and more what I was doing. First there was the new events manager he hired and the laundry list of proposed events and outreach they were brainstorming. Then he floated the idea of moving up the renovation on the second floor to get that ready for these grand plans, which I fully supported. Anything to bring in more paying customers, right? He also needed me to get working on the text for the tastings, approving what Douglas already had sketched out for the part-time tasting manager. Then I had the tour to plan and outline for Sean. And the water wheel renovation.

Maybe I had left too much in Sean's hands. The guilt was niggling at me and I was feeling left out of my own brewery, the one place I had been focused on for most of my life. Now I wondered if I even had a place as more then the guy who makes the beer? I knew Sean would never cut me out, but I had walked away again when I should be back there doing the hard work, the work I wanted to do.

I finished the calculations and saved the file. Then I opened the email and saw that it was from an address I didn't recognize. There was an attachment and for a minute, I thought it was spam, but it was labeled Jaxon and Sadie photo shoot. The email address now made sense. It was from Courtney. I clicked the attachment and my screen was filled with a picture of Sadie and me in the studio when we did the boudoir photo shoot.

Sadie was straddling me in a chair, my hands bracing her lower back. Sadie's head was thrown back, her hair falling like a wave behind her. The camera had been positioned behind Sadie, giving a perfect view from her face, down the valley of her perfect breasts where I was trailing kisses. The expression on both our faces was something I had never seen. Total bliss.

I clicked to the next image, and it was a later shot in the same sequence, Sadie still straddling me but gazing into my eyes. I could feel the electric connection between us, the moment where our souls united. It had nothing to do with sex. This was about an emotional connection, about two people in love.

I clicked through the rest of the pictures, my heart squeezing painfully as I relived the moment in stills. She even captured the love so clearly written on Sadie's face right after she told me she loved me. Courtney was brilliant. Fucking brilliant.

My cell phone rang. I picked it up without looking.

"You got the photos?" It was Sean.

"Yeah. Jesus. They're amazing." I could barely get the words out through my suddenly tight throat.

"Then why are you still in Germany?"

"Because I don't know what to do. No, that's not it," I corrected myself, finally willing to admit what I was really feeling. "I'm afraid. What if she hates me and refuses to see me?"

"That's a very real possibility. But the longer you stay away, the more likely it is that she will never give you a chance. You're in danger of losing her forever. What are you going to do?"

Fuck. I couldn't lose Sadie. She was my everything. I didn't know how I would win her back, but I would find a way.

"I'll call you with my flight details."

Sean chuckled. "I'll be waiting."

CHAPTER THIRTY-FIVE

SADIE

The bridesmaids had a final dinner gathering right after Thanksgiving to celebrate Chelsea's wedding. I broke the news that I had decided to go stag, and it went over about as well as expected. Which is to say, not well at all. After much persuading, arguing, and downright threatening, along with copious amounts of alcohol and some wild stories that may have included a turkey race that may have been a dream or a nightmare, I agreed to one last shot so I didn't destroy our chances of being shown up by the groomsmen at the wedding. I didn't want to lose to them, since they had been insufferable at the picnic in July. I couldn't let them win and think they were better than us. Not to mention none of us wanted to lose five hundred dollars or dance anything embarrassing at the Plaza. So I needed to find a date. Somehow.

The weekend after Thanksgiving was the Holly Creek historic home holiday tour. I usually loved the holiday house tour. It always got me into the Christmas spirit. Seeing all the old homes in Holly Creek, decorated for the season, inspired me. Each home picked a theme or a time period and decorated accordingly, then opened their home to the public for one afternoon and evening after Thanksgiving to let the public enjoy the spirit. They offered refreshments and a history of the home and the families who lived there. The town asked for volunteers to be stationed at each house to ensure no one got handsy or too intrusive for the homeowners.

I almost didn't volunteer this year. I didn't feel the holiday spirit and had been spending most of the past couple of weeks holed up in my house or my shop, working. Brooding was more like it, as my friends called it. I preferred to think of it as healing a broken heart but whatever it was called, I was a hermit.

And frankly, even I was getting sick of it and myself.

So I didn't argue too hard when Courtney insisted I volunteer this year and helped me pick an outfit for the festivities. I ended up in my bedroom with all my friends digging through my closet, pulling out dress after dress and evaluating them for sexiness and holiday theme appeal. Finally, they settled on one.

"This is perfect. The color is just right and you look amazing in it."

My heart stuttered. It was the same dress I'd worn the night Jaxon and I had our first date at the Chop House. I shook my head. "No, anything but that one."

"Trust me. Wear this one. You'll feel great and look even better," Lila cajoled.

I slipped it on, feeling the weight of the past settling on my shoulders along with the silk. But she was right. I loved this dress. It was time to reclaim it and its past for my own. And I looked fucking amazing in it.

"Okay, ladies. I'm ready. Let's do this thing."

Courtney grinned and we headed to the senior center where the tour assignments were being handed out. I was a little out of the loop since I had been holed up feeling sorry for myself. As a result, Mary Barrett, the mayor's wife had stepped up to coordinate this year's event. I'm sure she was thrilled since she always felt like her house had been slighted by the committee. And sure enough, her house was listed first on the tour route. I nudged Courtney who grinned and shrugged her shoulders. I only hoped Mary hadn't assigned me to work her house. It would be just like her to get a little payback.

By the time they got around to me, it was the tail end. She marched up to me, her hawk nose in the air and tried to peer down at me, even though I was taller. "Sadie, since you were late signing up, you got our last house. The Holden House. We don't have much of a write up on it, so improvise the best you can."

The Holden House? I always wanted that house every year but the Holdens usually handled it themselves and their daughter was their guide. But they were in South Carolina this year, the house closed up.

"I didn't think the Holden House was on the tour this year," I protested before she could walk away.

She narrowed her eyes. "If you can't handle it, I'll find someone else."

"No, I can handle it. I'm just surprised. Did they have a theme?"

She only stared then walked away. I sighed and looked at Courtney. "Shall we?"

Courtney and I headed to the Holden House. Holly Creek had received snow overnight, as if fate was conspiring to help us create the perfect winter wonderland. The town green sparkled in the moonlight, and, with the added lights that the town put up along the trees and the fences, it was gorgeous. The large evergreen in the center was decorated the previous Friday night in a tree lighting ceremony along with a carol sing, which my friends dragged me too, and it was magical. The evening reinforced why I loved Holly Creek and the season.

Courtney turned down Beaumont Street just off of Main and they headed for the Holden House. The whole street was lined with historic houses, most of them part of the tour and lit up for the evening event. And, at the end of the street, there stood the Holden House, a deep blue federal village style home with white accents. I really hadn't expected it, despite being assigned the house, but it was all lit up for the season. Courtney pulled around back in the driveway and we circled the sidewalk up front to the front door which was decorated with a gorgeous wreath.

I kept up a running commentary as we walked. "Did the Holdens come home for the season? They must have. They probably didn't want to be away from their kids for the holiday. I'm glad they're back. The tour wouldn't be the same without their house."

Courtney only nodded and knocked on the door. Since the tour hadn't officially started and wouldn't for another thirty minutes, we couldn't just walk in. As tour guides, we could get there early, familiarize ourselves with the set up so we could guide the visitors, but remember, this was someone's home so we had to be respectful, and remind our visitors of the same thing. I was eager to get inside and see how they decorated this year since they always chose something different every year.

But when the door opened, the decorations weren't what surprised me.

"What the hell are you doing here?"

CHAPTER THIRTY-SIX

JAXON

My heart seized when I heard the knock at the door. Lila had texted me that the game was afoot, or whatever code we had chosen for the evening. I assumed that meant they had gotten Sadie to agree to the tour and she was on her way to the house. Getting the girls on board was fairly easy, though I had to survive the grilling with lots of assurances that I had learned my lesson and I wasn't going to screw up again. Convincing Mary Barrett to add the Holden House to the list and assign it to Sadie was a little more complicated. I sensed there was some rivalry there, but her husband Zeke ran some interference and got it all sorted out.

Then we had to get the house ready. Sadie was the master at this, but, once I bought the house, the Holdens were happy to advise me on ideas for decorating. Their daughter even came down and helped me with some of the items in storage so I could be ready since I was late in preparing for the tour. Thank goodness they loved Sadie and would do anything for her.

When I heard the knock, I froze, then slowly walked to the door and opened it. Sadie stood with her back to the door, checking out the garland and lights woven into the cast iron fence. I cleared my throat and she slowly turned, her eyes widening.

She wore that sexy as fuck dress that had gotten my blood racing the first night we went out. I held my breath, hoping she wouldn't turn on those sexy heels and stride down the walkway and out of my life again, but she stayed frozen in place as if rooted there, staring at me. I took a chance and stepped forward, watching her carefully, hoping not to spook her. When she only stared at me, her eyes wide and uncertain, I tucked a lock of hair behind her ear.

"Sean was right. You haven't been sleeping well."

"But I lost weight. Not the weight loss program I'd recommend, but it beats all the others I've tried." She pasted on a smile, but it didn't reach her eyes.

I cupped her cheek. "You didn't need to lose anything. You're perfect just the way you are." I stepped back and gestured inside. "Your house tour awaits."

She narrowed her eyes. "I thought this was the Holden House. Where are the Holdens?"

I grinned sheepishly. "I believe they're still in South Carolina, where they're living. Unless they came up to see their kids for the holidays."

She followed me inside, not even noticing when Courtney slipped away with a wink to me. Sadie still looked spooked, and I didn't know what to say. We stopped in the front foyer in front of the main stairway, decorated with garland and holly and a small Christmas tree. Mistletoe hung from the ceiling above us but I wasn't about to take advantage and kiss her. The timing wasn't right. Not yet.

She stared around her, taking in the sights, then shook her head, tears in her eyes.

"Jaxon, what are we doing here? I can't do this again."

She turned for the door and I grabbed her hand, stopping her from leaving. "Sadie, wait. Please, hear me out. You were right. I put everything and everyone else first. I tried so hard to prove myself to everyone, to please everyone, that I forgot the most important person. You."

She shook her head, tears spilling down her cheeks. "No, I'm not the most important person, Jaxon. You should be the most important person. It doesn't matter what anyone else wants or tells you."

I pulled her close. "But you make me happy. If you're not happy, then neither am I. I spent the past ten years, longer really, trying to prove myself worthy of those big dreams and expectations that everyone had for me. First with football, then with a career, but none of it mattered if I didn't have the right person in my life. I don't care about any of it if I don't have you."

Hope was a faint glimmer in her eye, as if she wasn't sure she could trust it, wasn't sure she could believe. "You had me, Jaxon. For years, I was yours."

"And I was the damned fool who didn't treasure you. I wouldn't blame you if you walked away. I'm asking for one last chance. I promise you. I won't waste this one."

She chewed her lower lip, clearly torn. I picked up a ring box I had tucked away under the small arrangement of poinsettias on the table and handed it to her. Her eyes widened, and she took an involuntary step back.

"This better not be a ring."

I grinned. "No, we're not there yet. Consider this a down payment."

She frowned and opened the red velvet box. She gasped. "What is this?"

"It's the front door key to the Holden house. This house. I bought it, closed ten days ago. I'm putting down roots, Sadie. Right here in Holly Creek. Not only will I have a business here, but I have a home too. It might be too soon for you to trust me, but I'm asking for a chance, one more chance to prove to you that I love you and can be your soul mate, the partner you need and want in your life. Please."

Tears were streaming down her face freely now, but she ignored them, just stared at the key. "How did you keep this a secret for so long?"

I grinned. "There are a lot of people who love you and want you to be happy. Believe me, I had to run a gauntlet of people who tested me at every turn before helping me. I won them over. What about you?"

She looked around and spied the faces peering at us from the hallway and living room. Of course, we weren't alone, even if I tried to make it that way. There were too many people who wanted to be a part of this day who'd helped make it happen. Even the Holdens were here. Everyone was just waiting to see what Sadie would do.

She took a deep shuddering breath, then flung her arms around me, pulling me close. "I never stopped loving you, even when I wanted to. You're the other half of my heart, my soul mate. William Quinn was right. We belong together." She leaned back and peered up at me. "But I'm not moving in. Not yet."

I couldn't stop smiling. "That's fine, as long as you help me decorate. I'm hopeless at that. I needed a lot of help to pull this off."

"I've seen your room. Early thrift store. Not a chance. I'll handle decorating." She buried her face in my chest. "But I have one question for you."

"Anything, Sadie." I'd give her the world if I could.

"Would you be my plus one at my friend Chelsea's wedding in a couple of weeks?"

I burst out laughing as our friends joined our celebration.

EPILOGUE

SADIE

I sat at a small table in the corner of The Plaza Hotel Grand Ballroom, my feet in Jaxon's lap. He was massaging my instep, and I was moaning, though it could be from the insanely wonderful feeling of how he worked my sore feet or the delicious raspberry vanilla bean cake I was indulging in. I may make chocolate for a living and love it, but I can appreciate other flavors, and Chelsea had picked a truly wonderful cake for her wedding. An older couple wearing clothes that cost more than my car shot me a dirty look but I wasn't having sex at the table, though it may have sounded like it. I hoped they weren't anyone who could cause Chelsea any issues, though I suppose her new husband could defend her against any assholes in her new life if necessary.

The wedding had been beautiful, though I had never doubted it would be anything but that. Chelsea was gorgeous. Her groom, Rex, was impossibly handsome in his tux, thought I was partial to my plus-one, my brew master from upstate New York. Jaxon had given up Germany and his internship with a prestigious brewery to come home and be with me. I told him to go back and finish, but he refused, saying he knew what he needed to do to make Tap Meister a success. It was time to stop chasing after things and start doing. He wanted to live his own life and be a part of Tap Meister's future.

We were decorating the Holden house, though we were lucky. The Holdens had agreed to leave some of their antiques behind since they didn't fit with their lifestyle in South Carolina and their kids didn't want them. I'd just about died and danced a jig when they asked if we wanted them. I said yes before Jaxon could reply and reminded him of his promise that I could decorate. He smiled and just nodded. He was doing a lot of that lately. It wouldn't last. We'd have fights and argue like any couple, but we'd get through it.

"Your wedding favors are a big success," he rumbled from the chair next to me, his thumb hitting a particularly sore spot.

I had already had a few people come up to me and ask if I delivered to Manhattan and would make chocolate for their events. It was a nice side-benefit to making the wedding favors for Chelsea, and I still had the Valentine's Day event in Lovelorn and Theresa's wedding in the spring, also in Lovelorn. My little shop was growing. It was wonderful. I even had someone offer to invest in my shop if I wanted to expand to the city. No thanks. I was happy in my small town. Chelsea may have been the one to grow her wings in the city. This small town girl was perfectly content with her life. Though, I would investigate the shipping costs and logistics of catering events or shipping for select people, as needed.

"This cake is divine," I murmured as I licked the fork.

"I wouldn't know. You ate my slice," Jaxon pointed out, with bit of a pout.

I leaned forward and held out the fork with a bite on it. He closed his mouth over it and groaned. "That's almost as good as your chocolate. Or Hayes's Flourless Chocolate cake."

I frowned, disgruntled that I still hadn't wrangled the recipe out of him or his chef. "Don't remind me. Maybe the next time we eat at the Chop House, I'll figure it out. I've almost got it. I just can't figure out how his version isn't dry or heavy."

"He's getting suspicious. You've been there just about once a week this entire month and ordered it every time. He's going to ban you soon. And I'm not sure how close you are. The last attempt was truly dreadful."

I grunted. He wasn't wrong. It was beyond a disaster. My culinary school instructors would take back my certificates if they had tasted it. "I'll figure it out." The music shifted to a slow dance, and Jaxon slipped my shoe back on.

He stood and held out his hand. "Want to dance, Sadie?"

I smiled. I'd been waiting all night for this. Neither the bridesmaids or groomsmen had lost their bet so we hadn't had to do the embarrassing dance, thank goodness. I don't know if my feet could handle it in my shoes, to be honest. But, to dance with my handsome plus-one? That I could do, gladly, and suffer the pain of sore feet.

Jaxon drew me onto the dance floor, and it felt like we fit together like two puzzle pieces, a perfect match. I rested my head on his shoulder, feeling the steady beat of his heart next to my chest. He laid his cheek on my head, and we swayed gently to the music, our eyes closed, as the rest of the world drifted away, leaving us lost in our little world.

We stayed that way for several songs until my feet protested the uncomfortable shoes. No offense to Chelsea but this small-town girl was not made for big-city shoes or life. Give me sneakers and jeans any day. I finally pulled him aside and headed for our table, noting the crowd thinning out as the reception was nearing the end.

Jaxon tugged me close, kissing me deeply which quickly turned heated. I pulled back. "You know, the wedding is winding down. What do you say we take this party somewhere more private?"

A hotel bed that felt like a cloud and room service? A whole night with no one to bother us? Sign me up!

"What are we waiting for?"

Jaxon

I knew it was too soon for an engagement ring. Sadie had been very clear that she wanted to move slowly on that front. But I hated that we lived apart. Despite me giving her the house key when I came home, she had never used it. She said it was symbolic, more of a sign that I was moving back to town and staying, not that I wanted her to have complete access to my home. I needed to step it up if I wanted her to recognize how invested I was in our relationship.

The recipe was the perfect diversion. She'd been wanting that for months, and I had done everything but give Hayes a kidney to get it. I'm sure Sadie would have figured it out eventually, but I enjoyed giving this to her. And our deal guaranteed that Hayes would stock our beer, first shot at all our new brews, in the region. Win-win.

Now for phase two.

The morning after the wedding, we had brunch with the wedding party, then headed for home. It was Christmas Eve and we both had family obligations for the holiday. But more than that, we wanted to be home. I couldn't wait to spend Christmas with my niece and nephew, the first time I actually made it home for the holiday, and of course it would my first with Sadie as a couple since high school. Her parents were up from Florida for the holidays and she had already spent days baking cookies with her mom until I was sure I gained ten pounds just from the heavenly smells, though I did my share of taste testing too.

We got in late in the afternoon, thanks to the holiday travelers all doing exactly what we were—headed home for the season. Good thing we made no plans for Christmas Eve. I debated giving Sadie her present tonight but we're just too tired and I wanted to make sure she enjoyed it. So, we unpacked, wrapped some last minutes presents I picked up in the city for the family, and tumbled into bed.

The next morning, I woke before Sadie, amazingly. With her job, she was often up before me and was naturally an early riser, but the wedding and the festivities leading up to it wore her out. I eased out of bed reluctantly and slipped downstairs to the kitchen and the present I'd stashed just for this moment.

I took the box out of the refrigerator and arranged the contents on a tray with a carafe of coffee and two cups. I finished just in time to hear footsteps coming down the center stairway. I headed into the front living room with the tray and set it down on the round table in front of the couch just in time to see Sadie shuffle in the room, yawning.

"I can't believe I slept so late. The wedding completely exhausted me. When do we have to be at Lila's?"

She froze and her eyes widened at she took in me sitting at the table with the tray in front of me. "We have time for a special breakfast and some coffee to help wake you up."

She stumbled forward, falling to her knees on the other side of the table, her eyes fixed on the food I placed on the tray. "Is that what I think it is?"

I gestured to the envelope in front of the flourless chocolate cake that I just about gave up a kidney for and begged Lila to drop off for us. But what was in the envelope was even more costly.

Sadie pretended to shake it. "Well, it's not a new mixer. Too small. Or a ring. Too flat. I wonder what it could be. It can't beat the house I got earlier this month."

I grinned. "That wasn't your house. That was a down

payment on our relationship. There are steps to you getting it. We're still working through them."

She rolled her eyes. "Is this part two of the Jaxon Bigsly grand plan?"

I shrugged, not willing to give out my whole plan, not yet. "Open it and find out."

She was never one for waiting, so she eagerly ripped into the envelope, pieces falling around her until she stared at the piece of paper inside, her jaw slack. "Oh my God. How did you get this?"

"I won't even tell you what I had to promise him. But it was worth it. Now, you don't have to keep making me taste test your practice recipes. The last one was really dreadful and I haven't quite recovered yet. This is the real deal. Hayes's flourless chocolate cake recipe."

She sank back on her heels. "This might be better than a ring." She eyed me through her lashes, a smirk on her face. "Might be."

I couldn't help but grin. "Don't worry. Donut rings are for breakfast. I left them in the kitchen."

She burst out in laughter then dug into the piece of cake I already cut for her. "You'd better not expect me to share this with your family. Or mine for that matter. I'm keeping this for myself."

I reached for the knife and she playfully slapped my hand. "Mine."

"Fine. Maybe I won't give you your other present."

She narrowed her gaze at me. "Another present? I thought we said no presents this year since we were working on the house."

I grinned and stretched out under the fully decked out Christmas tree that Sadie and I had spent a very pleasurable afternoon decorating, then celebrating underneath in front of the dancing fire. I dug through the numerous presents for Lila and Tom's kids and pulled out the one I hid for Sadie. I passed her the long, flat box and she eyed me curiously.

"What is this?"

I shrugged. "Open it and find out."

She scowled but her joy at presents overrode her annoyance at me for not telling her, and she ripped into the gaily wrapped paper, shreds falling around her like snowflakes. She opened the box and cocked her head to the side.

"It's a welcome mat that says *Welcome to Sadie and Jaxon's Home*. What does that mean?"

I shifted across the floor so I was closer to her. Then I took her hands. "I gave you a key almost a month ago to the house. You probably thought it was symbolic. You specifically said you weren't ready for a ring or to move in. Maybe you still aren't, but I want you to live here, to move in with me. I love you, Sadie. I can't imagine my life without you in it. I want to wake up with you beside me. I want to see you at breakfast, talk with you over dinner, watch television with you at night. I want you by my side always. Maybe we're not ready for marriage, but I don't want you to go back to your place."

A slow smile spread across her face, along with something that looked like hope. "Countless times I've put that key in the lock to open the door but hesitated. I didn't want to push you, didn't want to presume, in case you weren't ready or had changed your mind. I was afraid that you would take it back. It helps that you bought the house of my dreams. So yes, I will move in with you. You can't get rid of me now."

"I wouldn't want to. You're my heart, my love. I need you by my side. I love you, Sadie Taylor. Thank you for sticking by me and giving me that second chance."

"Second chance? I think it was more like a third one, but who's counting." She grinned then cupped my cheeks in her hands and kissed me. "I'm so glad you decided to come home and pushed past my walls. I can't wait to build a life with you, Jaxon. I love you."

I kissed her, with all the love and emotion that I had in my heart, trying to show her how I felt, hoping she could feel how much she meant to me. When she pulled back, we were both breathing heavily, and I was checking out the space to see if we could christen the tree area again. I pulled her to me but she tugged free.

"Not yet. I have something for you." She rummaged around under the tree and pulled a small package out, wrapped in beautiful red paper and decorated with gold ribbon, looking much fancier than anything I could ever do.

It was almost too pretty to unwrap but I wanted to know what was inside. I tuned the ribbon off and gently loosened the paper, while Sadie rolled her eyes. "Just open it, already."

I smirked. "Patience, love. Good things come to those who wait. Or do you need another lesson in patience?"

She shuddered and blushed, remembering the night at the Plaza hotel where I demonstrated thoroughly how patience can be pleasurable, if a little frustrating. "Fine. Do it your way. But I'm going to eat more of the cake before I waste away."

I chuckled and tossed the paper aside, leaving a box. I opened the box and brushed aside the tissue. A picture was revealed. A gorgeous, sensual picture of Sadie, in black and white, wearing lingerie, looking pensive and oh so seductive and sexy and breathtakingly beautiful. My heart ached just looking at the gorgeous picture, revealing the amazing woman I knew she was.

I looked up to see Sadie watching me with trepidation. "You're fucking gorgeous and the sexiest woman ever. When did you have this taken?"

A shy smile curved her lips. "Courtney and I did a preliminary photo shoot the day we did the boudoir shoot, to help me get comfortable. I loved this one and thought you might like it."

"I love it, though no one else can see it." Now, where to put it where I could see it everyday but no one else would.

She bit her lower lip. "Well, that might be a problem. Courtney asked me if she could use it for a proposal she was working on for her business and I said yes."

I knew how sensitive Sadie was about her body. I took her hand and she looked at me. "Sadie, if you want to do this, I fully support you. You're gorgeous and I'm jealous as hell of anyone seeing you like this, but I would never stop you. I love you so much and am so fucking proud of you for doing this. Go for it, baby. You're amazing."

She blushed. "Courtney is the amazing one. She took the pictures."

I tucked my fingers under her chin and lifted her face. "Baby, she's a great photographer. That's true. But she had amazing material to work with. I love this picture but I love the real you even more. And it's been entirely too long since I've shown you."

I set aside the picture and took her piece of cake, despite her protest, and proceeded to show her how much I loved her.

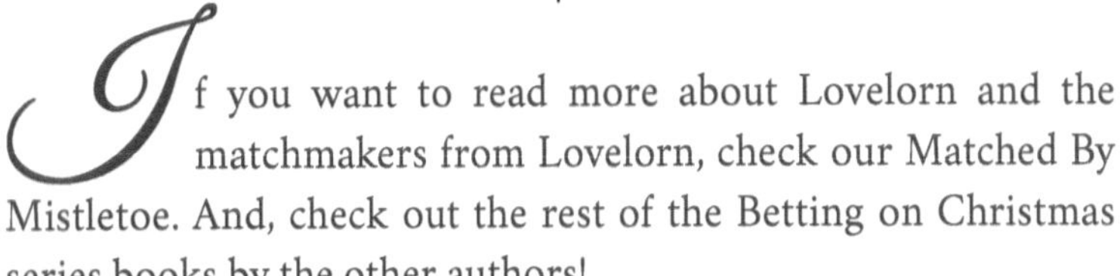

If you want to read more about Lovelorn and the matchmakers from Lovelorn, check our Matched By Mistletoe. And, check out the rest of the Betting on Christmas series books by the other authors!

A big city billionaire with a bride from a small town. A high society New York City wedding with a momzilla being bossy boots. And one crazy bet. Will the bridesmaids and groomsmen find their own dates to the wedding of the century this Christmas, or will they all fall victim to Mozilla's decree? Find out in these Betting on Christmas romances.

Prequel: Betting on Christmas - The Bet

The Bridesmaids

It Happened One Christmas - Zee Irwin

Who Needs A Boyfriend at Christmas - Delancey Stewart

Christmas & Other Inconveniences - Tracy Broemmer

Merry & Bright Christmas - Megan Ryder

Christmas with Her Fake Boyfriend - Kim Law

The Groomsmen

Mr. Grumpy's Christmas Date - Cat Johnson

He's Looking Like a Christmas Miracle - Amy Stephens

The Christmas Bargain - Peggy McKenzie

She's a Hot Christmas Mess - Sofia Aves

All I Want for Christmas is Her - Harper Cross

Want more of your favorite characters from the Betting on Christmas series? Well, your authors all have created BONUS EPILOGUES for you to revisit your characters and see how their stories continue. Click the link below or scan the QR code for the page of ALL the epilogues!

Click here for the epilogues or scan the QR code below.

ALSO BY MEGAN RYDER

THE KNIGHTS OF PASSION

The Knights of Passion. A team of sexy, dedicated men and women who love baseball and are filled with the competitive fire to win on the field and off the field. These are men and women who have been tested by life. They have found a place that they can call home and people they can call family.

Going All The Way (Knights of Passion 1)

Love From Left Field (Knights of Passion 2)

The Game Changer (Knights of Passion 3)

THE BRIDESMAIDS PROJECT

Three Bridesmaids. Three lost loves. One matchmaking bride. With just a week before the wedding, can a bride-to-be reunite her bridesmaids with the ones who got away?

Something Old

Something Borrowed

Something New

REDEMPTION RANCH

Welcome to Redemption Ranch, the place for second, third and even fourth chances, until you get it right. Meet Weston Morgan, Chase Summers and Ty Evans. Three foster brothers who found family, home and love at Redemption Ranch with their foster father Douglas Rawlings.

Set in the same town and world as Granite Junction, it's a prequel series to the Granite Junction series. You don't need to read it first but characters share between worlds.

A Cowboy's Salvation (Redemption Ranch 1)

Coming Home to the Cowboy (Redemption Ranch 2)

A Cowboy's Song (Redemption Ranch 3)

GRANITE JUNCTION SERIES

Welcome to Granite Junction, a spin off of the Redemption Ranch series, featuring characters we first met in Redemption Ranch and now get to have their own happy ever afters!

The Wrong Cowboy (Granite Junction 1) - Available now

The Restless Cowboy (Granite Junction 2) - Available now

A Cowboy to Remember (Granite Junction 2.5) - Available now

The Right Cowboy (Granite Junction 3) - Available now

The Rebellious Cowboy (Granite Junction 4) - Coming in 2023

ABOUT MEGAN RYDER

Ever since Megan Ryder discovered Jude Deveraux and Judith McNaught while sneaking around the "forbidden" romance section of the library one day after school, she has been voraciously devouring romance novels of all types. Now a romance author in her own right, Megan pens sexy contemporary novels all about family and hot lovin' with the boy next door. She's also a master procrastinator–if only her cocker spaniel, Bentley, would let her focus on writing instead of playing ball all day!

For a free book, upcoming releases and other information including access to bonus content, sign up for her newsletter at her website at https://www.meganryder.com

facebook.com/MeganRyderAuthor

x.com/MeganRyder1

instagram.com/meganryderauthor

amazon.com/Megan-Ryder/e/B010KHVU0G

bookbub.com/authors/megan-ryder

goodreads.com/Megan_Ryder